ACCIDENTAL
DIPLOMACY

JEFFREY BUSCH and DOMINIC MAN-KIT LAM

ARCHWAY
PUBLISHING

Archway Publishing books may be ordered through booksellers or by contacting:

Archway Publishing
1663 Liberty Drive
Bloomington, IN 47403
www.archwaypublishing.com
844-669-3957

ISBN: 978-1-6657-2997-0 (sc)
ISBN: 978-1-6657-2998-7 (hc)
ISBN: 978-1-6657-2999-4 (e)

Library of Congress Control Number: 2022916861

Print information available on the last page.

Archway Publishing rev. date: 09/20/2022

DEDICATION

Jeffrey Busch

This novel is dedicated to my daughters whom I love dearly. Gabrielle Busch and Samantha Busch Corsillo whom have given me great joy in my life.

Dominic Lam

This novel is dedicated to my mentors, children and grandchildren. They are often the sources of my inspiration & innovation, as well as my collaborators in art and science. With love and best Wishes.

ACKNOWLEDGMENT

We would like to thank the following for
their contribution to the novel.
Toby Osborne who joined Dominic and I to co-
write the screenplay this novel is based upon.
Logan Chipkin who provided great assistance to this novel.
Danica Holley for her valuable insight and input
Linda Libertucci for her valuable insight and input.
Mr. Alfred Law and Dr. Vanessa Li for
their advice and valuable input
Mr. Louis Lam for his Technical Assistance

ONE

★★★

CHAPTER

C ommander Wong looked out from the deck of a Chinese Navy ship. The vastness of the South China Sea always filled him with awe. His hand instinctively gripped one of the many medals around his neck as his eyes fell on the other ships adjacent to his own. Although each was built towards a unique purpose, the ships were uniform in their dreary, off-white sheen.

These waters are for China, the fifty-four-year-old thought as he stared at the navy. *Our people are older than the young, brash Americans who seek to infringe upon our birthright.*

Wong smiled and looked back out at the calm waters.

The commander's eyes narrowed as something glimmered on the horizon. "Commander Wong," a voice said from behind him, and he jumped in surprise. Wong turned around to see Officer Lu, a tall, handsome man. "We have report that a U.S. Navy battleship is approaching us. It's about eighty nautical miles to our west."

Wong's expression tightened. "Tell everyone to stay calm but keep their senses about them. Everything will be fine."

"Yes, sir."

As Officer Lu left Wong's side, the roar of engines filled the commander's ears. He looked up and saw three Chinese jet planes fly overhead and towards the glimmer that Wong had seen.

Admiral Smith stood in the U.S. battleship *Austin*'s control room, stern hands on his hips. At five feet, eight inches, he was not a large man, but his weathered face and authoritative gait more than compensated.

In the circular room, Smith was surrounded by blinking buttons, metallic switchboards, and half a dozen computer screens. He focused on a particular screen that revealed a trio of planes flying from the distance, growing larger by the second.

"Those are Chinese jets, sir!" Lieutenant Rodriguez said excitedly. "They're coming from the east, and they're heading in our direction!"

Smith gave the young lieutenant a hard look. "This is routine, son. There's no reason to be anxious. You have been well trained, and the Chinese do this often. They're just harassing us. Always stay calm, cool, and clearheaded. Remember that."

Admiral Smith turned to leave the control room. Just before he departed, with his back turned to Rodriguez, he said, "I'll brief the commander of the Pacific Fleet from my quarters. You stay put. Keep an eye on the Chinese, and talk to me before you take any action."

"Yes, sir!"

Pilot Hao Zhang gritted his teeth as he steered away from the U.S. Navy battleship at the last moment, taking a swift right-hand turn. Flying at the same altitude as the height of the ship, he had flown so close that he could make out the individual stars on the American flag that stood high on the ship's upper deck.

Zhang pressed a button on his cockpit control board and said, in perfect English, "Americans!" His voice emanated through radio waves, and he knew that the U.S. military could hear him. "Change course immediately! You are in Chinese waters!"

Lieutenant Rodriguez anxiously cracked his knuckles as he watched on the screens of the control room three Chinese jet planes skirt around the ship on which he stood. As they did, he heard Hao Zhang's warning come through the room's speakers. *Stay calm, stay calm*, he thought to himself. Rodriguez picked up a microphone of his own and turned it on. After a few tense seconds of connecting his signal to that of the three pilots, he replied, "This is USS *Benfold*. We are conducting a freedom of navigation operation in international waters. We have as much of a right to be here as you do. Stand down! I said, 'Stand down!' Hello? Can you hear me!"

Hao Zhang circled the U.S. battleship like a patient shark. He frowned as he heard the American's order to leave. *He does not have the authority to do that*, he thought in a frenzy. *These are our waters.*

The pilot flicked two adjacent switches in front of him. "Zhu, Tan, can you hear me?" he said into his microphone.

"Yes."

"Copy."

Zhang eyed the U.S. battleship from his side as he swung around it. He saw the other two Chinese jets in the distance, similarly circling the ship. "Ready your missiles to show them that we are serious, but do not fire. We need to scare them a little."

Lieutenant Rodriguez's eyes widened as he saw the Chinese jet planes prepare for attack. They were far enough apart from each other that each jet plane was on a unique screen. Rodriguez shifted his attention between them every half second, which only served to increase his heart rate.

Holy shit, he thought. *They're actually going to fire.*

He looked at the several other officers around him, all of whom looked nervous, as this was not a routine flyby.

Admiral Smith was working in his quarters when his assistant announced that he had an incoming call from the chief computer engineer, Raymond.

"Hello?" Smith grunted.

"Sir, it's Raymond. I just wanted to let you know that we've found a bug in our computer control system."

"What does that mean?" Smith asked.

"It is now possible for us to receive false signals. This will take an hour or two to fix."

Smith cursed. "Please notify the control room, ASAP."

"Yes, sir."

A warning light turned on in the room, which Rodriguez knew indicated that missiles had been activated.

He ran to the room's phone and dialed. "Hello?" said a voice that the lieutenant did not recognize.

"Hi, this is Lieutenant Rodriguez. Please connect me to Admiral Smith! It's an emergency!"

"I'm sorry, he's on another—"

"put him on the phone, now!" Rodriguez yelled. "Jesus, we don't have time!"

As his breathing quickened, the young lieutenant noticed that the three Chinese planes were no longer circling the ship.

They were closing in on it.

"H-hello?" he said into the phone.

"Yes, sir. I'm connecting you to Admiral Smith now. I do apologize for the delay. It'll only be a few more seconds."

Rodriguez shook his head as he looked at the red warning light that indicated that a missile was locked on the ship and ready to be fired. He looked up and saw several Chinese jets closing in.

No time, he thought with grave but disciplined concern.

"Fire!" one of the nearby officers barked.

Rodriguez hung up the phone and froze.

"What are you doing?" another officer yelled. "Launch the missile, or we are going to die!"

The phone started ringing, but Rodriguez ignored it. Like jumping into a cold pool, he reached his right hand out to the control center's smallest switchboard, pulled back the glass off a large button, and pressed it.

Someone yelled, "The chief engineer!"

But it was too late.

Zhang did not have time to react. One second he and his comrades were closing in on the U.S. Navy battleship. The next, two angry missiles thundered from the ship's missile launcher. Although smoke blurred the scene, he saw from his jet's left panel that one of the missiles twisted and turned through the air until it collided with Zhu's plane. Zhang's jaw dropped in disbelief as he heard two simultaneous explosions—although he watched Zhu's plane explode in a sphere of fire, pilot Tan must have met the same fate.

What is this? Zhang thought. He throttled his joystick so that his plane rose to a higher altitude. He soared over the U.S. battleship as he deliberated what to do next.

Lieutenant Rodriguez had to consciously force his hands to stop shaking. He tried counting his breaths in order to calm down, but he could not get beyond three before his stomach flipped in revulsion. He swallowed so as to prevent himself from vomiting.

Suddenly, a voice came through the phone that he was still holding to his ear. "Rodriguez!" Admiral Smith shouted angrily. "Are you there? Rodriguez!"

"Yes, sir!" the lieutenant replied.

"What in the hell did you just do?"

"Sir," Rodriguez said between nearly hyperventilated breaths. "T-they were about to attack us! I … I protected us."

Smith uttered a chain of curses, most of which were directed at Rodriguez. "Don't you move another goddamned muscle. You are hereby relieved from your post. Jesus, Rodriguez! Do you even understand what you've done?"

Rodriguez tried to talk, but nothing came out. He put the phone down and fell to the floor in utter despair.

Commander Wong made his way into his navy ship's command center, where he watched satellite video of two Chinese jets exploding at the hand of American missiles. Officer Lang, who was sitting at the control panel, spun his chair around to face Wong. Each held a somber expression.

"They killed pilots Zhu and Tan!" Lang cried.

Wong nodded. "Yes, they did."

Lang put his hands up in exasperation. "What should we do?"

"Nothing. Tell Zhang to return to base. Immediately."

Officer Lang did not seem satisfied, but he took his order in stride. He attempted to radio the surviving pilot. After a moment, Lang said, "He's not responding, commander!"

These Americans think that they can exploit China and push us around, Zhang thought to himself as he steered his jet plane back towards the U.S. battleship. *Time to change that.*

Wong and Lang watched as pilot Zhang headed towards the Americans. Commander Wong rushed to grab the radio that Lang had held and yelled, "Zhang! I order you to stand down! Do not engage! I repeat, do not engage!"

Inside his cockpit, Zhang flicked a switch while his eyes never left his target, the great navy battleship in front of him. *This is for you, my fallen brothers.*

And a deadly missile rocketed through the air.

Rodriguez was still on the ground when the door to the command center flew open. He heard footsteps from multiple sources, but he did not bother to look up.

"Grab him and throw him in the brig!" Admiral Smith barked. "And when you're finished, send China a message: this was an accident. And you, get me the secretary of defense on the line, pronto."

While two officers pulled Rodriguez to his feet, one of them pointed at the screens and said, "Admiral! Missile incoming!"

Their world rocked as if struck by an earthquake. The four men were thrown around the room as a terrifying *BOOM!* filled their eardrums. Rodriguez's back slammed against the wall, and agony flooded him even as fear and confusion overtook his rational mind. A few seconds later, the world stood still again, and only the sound of alarms filled the void. Rubble filled the room as bits and pieces of the command center's technological devices fell from the walls and the ceiling.

The battleship was listing on its starboard side and heading into the water.

"Abandon ship!" Admiral Smith said, already returning to his feet.

Commander Wong watched as his pilot's missile struck the side of the U.S. battleship, exploding in a mess of fire and metal. The still waters around the ship broke into violent waves as the American battleship shuddered from the blast.

Wong's expression was granite as he contemplated the consequences of his pilot's defiance.

TWO
★ ★ ★
CHAPTER

S ecretary of State Bill Bryers walked onto the beautiful, historic Georgetown University Quad. The sixty-three-year-old stood with his hands on his sides, tall and self-assured. With short dark hair, a waistline that hadn't grown since he was in his twenties, and an American flag button pinned to his navy jacket, his line of work wouldn't surprise anyone.

I love this place, he thought whimsically. *It's nearly as old as the United States itself, having been established in 1789. It's a shining light on the hill, a leading educating institution of U.S. leaders. Two presidents have graduated from here, along with numerous senators, congressmen, international royalty, and fourteen foreign heads of state.*

As he continued to walk, Dean Longworth, the head of the foreign service school, darted across campus to greet him.

"Bill," he began, "I hear you're going to stop teaching your seminar after this semester. Twenty-five years you put in!"

Bill nodded with a proud smile. "You heard right. I'll miss it a lot. I love teaching, and I love hearing from my students. Frankly, I often learn as much as they do during our time together. But what can I say—my wife, daughters, and doctor are telling me to cut down on my activities. Maybe I can continue teaching once I'm no longer secretary of state."

"Do as you must," the dean responded, "but in the meantime, you will be missed."

"Thank you, sir."

Just as the dean walked away, two students approached Bill. The secretary of state recognized them.

"Gayle and Stuart!" Bill exclaimed amicably. "What can I do for you?"

"Can we walk with you to class?" Stuart asked nervously.

Bill chuckled. "Of course you can, I'd love the company. Stuart, how is your master's thesis going?"

Stuart pulled out a thick packet of laminated paper. "Here's the latest draft. Care to take a look?"

Bill accepted the work and glanced at the title on the front page: 'Diplomatic approaches to stop the inevitable war between the United States and China.' He handed it back to the student. "Sounds interesting," Bill said. "Send it to me, I'll take a look."

"Thank you, professor! Will you know how to download the file?"

Bill laughed. "Of course. I'll read it over the weekend."

A few minutes later, the trio arrived in the seminar room 11-A. Bill glanced between his watch and the sea of quiet young minds in the crowd before him. He clasped his hands together in a thunderous but friendly gesture. "Good morning, to my favorite master's class."

Bill turned away from his students, grabbed a marker, and wrote on the blackboard beside his podium: *Do superpowers inevitably go to war or not?*

The secretary of state capped his marker and returned to face the class.

Bill cleared his throat and pointed to one of his students, Susan. "Before we start, I'd like to congratulate Susan on her marriage."

After the class finished applauding, Bill asked, "May I ask, where did you go for your honeymoon?"

Susan blushed and said, "Thank you, professor. It's so kind of you to remember. We went to Italy for ten days!"

Bill laughed with joy. "Now, let's get down to business. You all are working on your master's thesis on how diplomacy affects whether two superpowers go to war. Each of you were assigned a case study in which two or more superpowers confronted each other, and how diplomacy either successfully led to the avoidance of war, or its failure led to war.

"Some of you don't yet have master's thesis topics. I think a great one would be the hundreds of years of conflict between the Ottoman Empire, which controlled most of the Middle East, and the Habsburg Empire, which controlled much territory in Europe. This is a great example of good communications and diplomacy preventing these powers from engaging in constant war over two hundred years. However, eventually they *did* go to war. What went wrong? Contact me if you want this as your thesis topic. It's a great prelude to some of the successes in the Cold War, and also to later failures like World War I.

"Speaking of World War I, this was a classic case of miscalculation, secret and public treaties, mutual defense pacts, and poor diplomacy. All of these factors contributed to the resultant major war that most countries did not want. Carlos, since you're writing your thesis on World War I, would you like to tell us how it began, and what we can learn from it?"

A skinny student towards the front spoke up. "Throughout history, there have always been mutual defense agreements that have caused war between otherwise friendly nations. With respect to World War I, there were treaties between Russia and Serbia, Germany and Austria-Hungary, France and Russia, Britain and Belgium, and Japan and Britain."

"It should be noted," Bill added, "that the United States was not part of this network of treaties."

"It was like a game of dominos, even without those two superpowers," Carlos continued. "The prince of Austria-Hungary was assassinated in Serbia. Then Serbia gave into Austria-Hungary's peace demands but was attacked by the much larger Austria-Hungarian Empire, anyway. Russia came to Serbia's defense, and Germany joined Austria-Hungary's side. As a result, Germany and Russia, though not initially in conflict, went to war. Eventually, France and Britain joined Serbia and Russia. All in all, the war cost twenty million deaths and another twenty-one million casualties of war."

"Very good, Carlos," Bill said. "I want you to also focus more of your thesis on the diplomatic efforts involved. You can see that, once a war starts, it is very difficult to stop. World War I was started via unintended consequences. A dispute between two countries and mutual defense treaties forced superpowers that had been intertwined through treaties into the very deadly conflict of World War I. This is a clear example of a war that could have been prevented by good diplomacy. The countries miscalculated when they entered the war, thinking that it would be a short and limited war. As we learn from history, wars rarely go as planned. Death and destruction usually end up far worse than what we predicted."

Bill peered at his notes and looked back up at the class. "Moving on to Samantha. You are studying World War II for your thesis. You all know about Hitler's infamous invasion of Poland that began a chain reaction that was similar to that of World War I. But before the invasion of Poland, there was diplomacy with Germany. Agreement was reached with Hitler. Even the English prime minster, Neville Chamberlain, famously declared that 'there will be peace in our time.' Except there wasn't. He gave in to Hitler's Germany, even though Hitler was not to be trusted. Samantha, your paper should focus on how the diplomatic efforts failed."

A very bright blonde student sitting on the last seat at the end of table 18-A said, "Hitler broke his promise to Chamberlain and invaded Poland. England and France declared war on Germany, since they were allies of Poland. Then Germany invaded France, and England sent troops to aid France. We all know how this story ends. The Allied powers of Great Britain, the United States, the Soviet Union, China, and, to a lesser extent, France, came together and defeated the Axis powers of Germany, Italy, and Japan. There were far more than two powers during World War II, making it another outlier in our list of historical examples."

"In short," Bill said, "poor diplomatic negotiations that tried to appease Hitler and Germany contributed to a devastating war. Sometimes, the best diplomacy is to be tough with the aggressor so that there are no misunderstandings about your intentions. England and France allowed Germany to take sovereign countries such as Czechoslovakia. When Germany invaded Poland, Hitler thought that they would back down again. We will never know if an earlier strong stance by England and France would have avoided war. Samantha, I hope that your thesis looks into that issue."

Bill said, "Moving on, then. After Hitler and Germany surrendered, Russia and her allies faced off against the United States and her allies in the Cold War."

Bill paused to clear his throat. "Now, let's hear from Gabriella about the Cold War."

Another beautiful, bright young woman with pretty blue eyes and brown hair in the back smiled and said, "I just want to say that this war was a diplomatic success. Finally, it's a case for good diplomacy."

The class laughed, as did Bill.

"Well," Bill said, "this *is* a class in diplomacy, after all. The class in war history is probably down the hall."

The entire class laughed.

Gabriella said loudly, "The Cold War lasted from 1947, the year of the Truman Doctrine, to 1991, the year that the Soviet Union dissolved. The conflict also roped in the allies of both the United States and the Soviet Union, dubbed the Western Bloc and Eastern Bloc, respectively. Although there was no violence between the two superpowers, they did *cause* violence by way of proxy wars."

Bill nodded. "Thanks, Gabriella. Since both sides had nuclear weapons, a war may have caused mutually assured destruction between the United States and the Soviet Union. This meant that the diplomatic summits between leaders were critical to maintaining the peace. After Russia and the United States almost went to war over the Cuban missile crisis, they even installed a direct telephone line between the two leaders.

"Because each side knew that the other one held nuclear weapons, both were very wary of attacking the other. This delicate peace predicated on knowledge of the other's ability to ravage the entire planet was known as mutually assured destruction. Instead of direct fighting, the two powers engaged in propaganda, espionage, and trade wars. The tension between them even spilled out into sports and technological competition. I'll talk next class about the end of the Soviet Union."

Bill swallowed before continuing. "While the United States and the rest of the Western Bloc were mostly liberal democracies, the Soviet Union was dominated by Russia. Each power supported client governments with which it shared a political ideology. Amy, you're researching the origins of NATO. Can you please tell the class more about how it was started?"

"Definitely," a cheery woman in glasses said. "In 1949, the United States created the NATO military alliance that aimed to contain Soviet influence around the world. The Soviet Union, meanwhile, established the Warsaw Pact in 1955. The two states competed for influence in Latin America, the Middle East, and elsewhere. But constant diplomacy through diplomatic channels and summits between leaders allowed for a devastating World War III to be avoided."

"Thank you," Bill said. "Okay, Stuart. Please give us a summary of your report on the current tension between the two contemporary superpowers, the United States and China. Please be quick, as we're running out of time."

A heavyset man towards the room's right-hand side spoke up. "Although history tells us that there is an inevitable war between the United States and China on the horizon, I think that there is a possibility of peaceful coexistence, much like there was during the Cold War."

"Very interesting," Bill said. "China has a massive naval and military buildup because of territorial issues in the South China Sea and Taiwan. Plus, it feels surrounded in the Pacific by U.S. allies. This includes Japan, South Korea, Taiwan, and the Philippines. China already has a navy that is larger than America's, although it's still far less powerful."

Suddenly, the doors to the lecture hall opened, and three well-dressed men rushed in. One of them ran towards Bill and whispered in his ear, "Bill, we have a major international crisis. I need to take you to the White House right away."

Bill kept his composure and walked with the three men. Just as he left the hall, he announced to his class, "I'll see you next week!"

CHAPTER
THREE
★ ★ ★

South China Sea

Commander Butcher squinted at the open sea.

"Kenny!" he barked, never taking his eyes off of the object that was gradually coming into view.

"Yes, sir?"

Commander Butcher pointed out towards the open waters.

Kenny released an audible gasp. "We found survivors!"

Butcher turned to his subordinate. "Tell the captain. They could be Americans."

Kenny nodded and wordlessly heeded the command.

Commander Butcher stood in silence for a good while. Finally, as the ship came into close proximity with the raft, he looked down and saw twelve navy members. He recognized one: the famous Admiral Smith.

Butcher ran over to the side of the ship, where his crew was already beginning to hoist Smith and his fellow travelers from their raft. Butcher pushed his way to the very edge of the ship and began helping with his own hands.

Once all twelve men were safely on the ship, Butcher went to help Admiral Smith stay on his feet. Smith's clothes were torn up, and his face was dirty and bruised.

"Admiral," he said quickly. "Can you talk? What the hell happened?"

Smith looked at him with tired eyes. "You'll hear about it soon enough. The long and short of it is, we got into it with the Chinese not far from here."

"My god," Smith whispered to the captain. "How many men and women did we lose?"

"From what I know, at least ninety-two are dead, and over sixteen hundred are missing. There is a full-scale rescue effort going on."

Butcher cursed. "How did this happen?"

Admiral Smith's eyes narrowed. "That's the question."

"I see lots of rafts and men in the water, over there!" Butcher yelled with excitement.

"Send out rescue boats and helicopters to pick them up," the captain replied.

White House, Washington, D.C.

As the town car pulled up to the White House, the Secret Service agents at the security gate quickly opened it for Bill. They did the same for the secretary of state at the entrance to the West Wing. At last, the secretary of state was ushered into the president's office.

"We have a major international crisis with China," the president said to Bill.

Bill remained calm and professional. "How bad?"

"Not all of the information is in, but it appears that we accidentally shot down two of their planes that were harassing our fleet."

"In international waters?"

"Yes," the secretary of defense replied. "But China claims the territory because it is within one hundred and seventy-four nautical miles of their man-made islands. So they struck back and sunk a battleship."

"Which battleship?" Bill asked.

"The *Austin.*"

"Oh my god," Bill breathed. "My son-in-law serves on that."

"We have many survivors," the secretary of defense assured Bill. "I will let you know about your son-in-law's status. Bill, you and I both read the daily national security memos. China is clearly expanding its territorial claims and rapidly expanding its military budget. We have the number one military budget in the world, but China is second. China's budget is three times larger than numbers three and four, India and Russia. United with Russia, China would be a formidable adversary."

"I agree."

"I don't want war with China," the president said, "but if we must fight, we will. I am sending two aircraft carrier strike groups into the South China Sea. Bill, you need to use your diplomatic skills to settle this matter."

"Okay, I will head back to the State Department now."

Bill sat down in his U.S. State Department office on a cool autumn morning, holding a travel mug in his hand. He briefly looked around the room and took a moment to embrace the comfort that its familiarity brought him. Any of Bill's close associates would have recognized the room immediately as Bill's. On its right side stood a tall cabinet divided into four bookshelves, all filled with books about history, political theory, and law. The wall opposite the bookshelves was decorated with two large paintings, one of the Rocky Mountains and one of an American flag waving before a teal blue sky. A gray statue of the Roman statesman Cicero stood a few inches in front of the paintings, its face pensive.

The secretary of state grabbed the remote control on his desk and turned on the television that hung on the far side of his office. His preferred twenty-four-hour news network came to life with the volume on low. A headline read across the screen as a news anchor spoke: "NAVAL BATTLE BETWEEN U.S. AND CHINA."

Bill frowned, but then his phone buzzed in his pocket. He turned away from the television, took out his phone, and read the name "Admiral Lucas Smith" on the screen.

"Good morning, Admiral," Bill said softly as he put the phone to his ear. "Update me on the situation."

"Not good, Secretary Bryers," Smith replied gruffly, before sighing audibly. "Today is a tragic day for us and for them, Secretary. Mistakes were made over the South China Sea. It is clear that our guys shot down two of their planes. He panicked over a false signal. They responded in kind. We have lots of casualties from our sunken battleship. I know that your son-in-law was an officer on that ship."

"Any news about him?" Bill asked anxiously.

"Not yet. We are still searching the waters and finding survivors."

Bill swallowed but kept his composure. "Tell me something I won't hear on the news."

"The fight is on, Secretary."

"What? What does that mean?" Bill asked.

"The president has ordered two aircraft carrier strike groups to head to the South China Sea and cross into the disputed areas. We hear from the CIA that China plans to create a red line in the South China Sea such that if we cross it, there would be a state of war."

There was a *beep* over the phone, and a third voice said, "Alan Parsons here. Bill, Lucas. Morning."

The secretary of the navy? Bill thought worriedly to himself. "Mr. Secretary."

"Hello, Mr. Secretary," Smith aped.

"Bill, has Lucas brought you up to speed?" Parsons asked.

"He was in the middle of doing so," Bill answered. "Though I think I get the picture. Are we headed to war, or can we prevent the worst?"

"This is a ripe opportunity for us," Parsons said. "We can show the Chinese that we mean business. If they want a fight, we'll give them one."

"Maybe they *don't* want a fight," Bill said sharply. "Diplomacy has worked for us in the past. There's no reason it can't work again."

"Yes, there is, Bill," Admiral Smith growled. "The Chinese look out for themselves and only themselves. They're sharks in the water. You don't negotiate with predators. You exterminate them."

Bill clenched his jaw. "I insist on diplomacy, Admiral. When we *can* avoid bloodshed, we should."

"The history books would mock such naïve efforts," Smith said.

Bill shook his head angrily. "We're trying diplomacy first." Suddenly, Bill heard a knock on his office door. "I have to go. Admiral Smith, Secretary Parsons, respectfully, we *will* talk with the Chinese before anyone else is killed. We will reconvene soon. Take care."

The secretary of state hung up the phone and shouted, "Who is it?"

"It's Shelly, sir," a gravelly but female voice said from the other side of the door.

Bill relaxed a little. Shelly was one of his advisors, and one whom Bill liked very much. "Please, come in!"

A tall, thin woman in her late thirties entered the office, holding a plain folder. She briskly approached Bill's desk and handed it to him, her red curls bounding over her shoulders the entire way. Bill nodded gratefully to her and gestured for Shelly to take a seat.

"Thanks, Shelly," Bill said. "While you're here, I have something for you, as well." He reached into a drawer beneath his desk and pulled out a gift basket covered in shrink wrap. A red envelope was taped onto the basket's top. "It's been a great ten years working with you, Shelly. You've really come into your own."

Shelly's narrow features lifted at once in elation. She looked Bill in the eyes and said, "You remembered!" She took the gift basket and placed it by her feet. "That's so kind of you. The pleasure's been all mine, Bill. Your mentorship's meant the world to me."

Bill smiled. "I just can't believe you put up with me for so long."

The two laughed. For a moment, the growing anxiety in Bill's mind faded into the background as he enjoyed a moment with his mentee and friend.

"Alright, well, I just wanted to give you that briefing," Shelly said.

Bill blinked. He had not even asked about the contents of the folder. *Focus, focus ...* he told himself. "Right. Thank you, Shelly."

As his advisor left, Bill read the folder's heading, which was typed in a font almost too small to be noticeable: "National Security Briefing." Bill swallowed again and opened it.

Beijing

Foreign Minister Yao Sheng sat at his desk, frowning as he shuffled through a mountain of papers. In his late sixties, nearly bald, and wearing a formal black suit and glasses, he emanated stern purpose to anyone who might have passed him a glance. As he sifted through his papers, emails, and phone messages, Yao mused to himself, *No more multitasking anymore. You're too old for it.*

Finally, he found the letter that he had been searching for. One long paragraph was handwritten on very expensive paper, with his handwritten signature at the bottom. He began reading his resignation letter to China's president to himself, as he had several times in the last few months.

I have tried to continue to fulfill my duties as Foreign Minister during my one hundred days of mourning since the loss of my wife. But I am not the man I thought I was. The aches of my heart have spread, tumor-like, to my mind, and my work has suffered for it. I love my country dearly, and I thought that I would be able to muster the discipline that China requires of me to be an effective statesman. I was mistaken. My love for China has not been enough to fill the void left by my dead wife. My family needs me now more than ever. For these reasons, it would be in the country's best interests for someone else to—

A long *buzz* from the office's intercom interrupted Yao's reading. He looked up and said, "Hello?"

"Mr. Sheng," his assistant said. "The minister of national defense is on the line."

Yao wiped his face with tired hands. Then he rose from his seat, walked towards the center of the room, and began pacing with his hands behind his back. The minister of national defense, General Shi Li, was not one for lighthearted conversation. "Please, put him through."

"Minister Sheng," boomed a deep, authoritative voice from the intercom, "the Americans attacked us in the South China Sea. They shot down two of our planes. Both pilots died."

Yao turned around as he reached one of the office walls and continued pacing about.

"They were on *our* waters," Shi continued. "So we sank the attacking battleship. And now we may be at war with the Americans. They are sending two aircraft carrier groups to confront us as we speak."

"Who authorized the retaliation?" Yao asked.

"It was unauthorized. But this is irrelevant. The Americans came to *us* and slaughtered our brethren. *They* violated protocol."

Yao's weathered face wrinkled in fury. "Unauthorized? Are you serious?"

"Yao. They attacked us. On our waters. A few hundred miles from Hainan. Imagine what Americans would do if our fleet was a few hundred miles from San Diego. I am sure they would take action."

"We sank a U.S. battleship!" Yao yelled. "Justified or not, we are going to face monumental consequences." Yao returned to his desk in seething silence. He grabbed the note that he had been reading. It was to be his resignation letter. It was to be his final words of appreciation to the people of China whom he had served for so long. It was to be his liberation from his stressful world.

Yao Sheng crumpled the paper in his fist and tossed it into the wastepaper basket.

"This could start World War III!" he shouted.

"The chairman of the Central Military Commission is sending a fleet to meet them," Shi responded stoically. "If they want war, we'll make it cost them. *We are declaring a red line in the South China Sea that they shall not cross!*"

In anger, Yao slammed both palms onto his desk so hard that two of its legs snapped, and the entire desk collapsed. Yao took a few surprising steps back as chaotic noise filled his ears.

"What was that?" Shi asked.

"Nothing," Yao whispered as he got his breathing under control.

"Listen, Yao. This is happening. We'll be in touch." A *click* signaled to Yao that Shi had hung up.

Yao stood in place for an entire minute. *I'm so sorry*, he thought, envisioning his family. *For the sake of China, I cannot be there for you.*

He grabbed the television remote control from the debris that was his desk and turned the volume up on his office television. A BBC news anchor was speaking, and she looked disconcerted. "We have breaking news. A U.S. Navy battleship was attacked in the South China Sea by the Chinese jet. This was in response to the Americans shooting down two Chinese jets. Internet rumors abound in the hour since the incident …"

Yao rubbed his face in worry. *I hope we can prevent a war. I have to negotiate with the U.S. secretary of state, Bryers. I* really *hate him, and he hates me. But my primary duty is to prevent war.*

FOUR
★★★
CHAPTER

Washington, D.C.

Bill removed his glasses to rub his eyes, an instinctive gesture of worry. He stood in the middle of his office, fixated.

"The U.S. president has issued a statement regarding the ongoing crisis with China," the news anchor began. "He will send two aircraft carrier groups to confront China. He will, and I quote, 'show them our military might.'"

The secretary of state muttered curses under his breath. He opened and closed his hands as a feeling of helplessness overcame him. Then he shook his head.

There must be a peaceful way out of this.

Beijing

As Yao stared at the ruins that were once his desk, his office telephone began to ring from a spot on the ground. The man tiptoed around the debris, leaned down, and picked up the phone.

He swallowed before answering, gathering himself together. "Yes?"

"Mr. Sheng, it's me again," the assistant said. "Are you free?"

Good question, Yao thought. *Am I?* "I have time now. What's going on?"

"The United States secretary of state, William Bryers, is on the line. He wants to speak with you."

Yao nodded. "Okay. Please put him through."

After a *beep*, Yao heard, "Hello, is this Foreign Minister Sheng?"

"Yes. Hello, Mr. Secretary." *Again*, Yao thought. "Thank you for calling me. And may I call you Bill?"

Yao heard a sigh from the other end. "I'd rather us be more formal. Call me Secretary. And I imagine that you've heard the news by now."

Yao thought he heard a bit of sarcasm, but he let it go. "I have heard. A tragic battle between our countries. Your ships should not have been in Chinese waters!"

"I think we should meet, Minister Sheng," Bill said.

Yao's heart beat faster. *Perhaps he wants war as little as I do. There is hope, yet.* "That is the wise course of action."

"I'm glad we agree on that, at least."

"Are you able to come here?" Yao asked. *If not, I'll know you're not interested in a good-faith attempt at keeping the peace. The incident occurred in* our *waters, after all.*

"Absolutely," Bill answered.

Yao breathed out in complete relief. "Thank you for understanding, Mr. Secretary. I'm glad you're willing to travel to China. My colleagues will take it as a sign that you know that it was America's fault. I will ensure that our commander, Wong, attends our peace talks."

"Minister, with all due respect, the incident was *not* our fault. Your planes had been testing us daily. An accident was waiting to happen because of choices made on *your* end."

Yao picked up the phone from its mount so that he could stand up. "What? Accept responsibility, Secretary. The regrettable errors in America's judgment undermine trust between our governments."

"Look, let's not let talks spiral out of control. Diplomatic efforts will not be limited to conversations between you and me. Please, let's drop it."

Yao breathed and closed his eyes before answering. "For now, alright. War must always be a last resort. Should bullets fly following this tragedy, you and I will both have failed in our duties."

"Yes," Bill agreed, and his tone indicated to Yao that he wanted the subject dropped.

"How soon can you be in Beijing?" Yao asked.

"As soon as you'll have us."

Yao pursed his lips in contemplation. "Excellent. Our delegates should meet for a summit, where we can talk about these matters in person. I can't officially confirm until I speak with my superiors, but we should be ready to receive you in twenty hours."

"Good, good," Bill said. "I look forward to your confirmation. I'll have my team ready. We can be there."

"Thank you, Secretary Bryers. I will speak with you soon."

Yao hung up the phone in his mess of an office.

We have one shot at peace, he thought to himself. *But there is hope. We can avoid war. I really just dislike Secretary Bryers, and I don't trust him. He has never been a friend of China.*

I have been teaching the Ministry that traditional Chinese values should be incorporated into China's foreign policy. These values are the key to resolving conflict. The values of harmony, benevolence, righteousness, courtesy, wisdom, honesty, and loyalty must all be part of the negotiations.

The Pentagon

Admiral Smith, who just returned from the South China Sea, strutted down the long corridor in full military garb and a scowl on his red face. With him walked Joint Chief Admiral Curtis Watkins, a fifty-two-year-old of medium stature, with short red hair and wild blue eyes.

"I've said it before, and I will repeat myself until God himself hears me. The Chinese gotta learn their damn place!"

"You don't think you're playing with fire, Admiral?" Watkins asked nervously.

"Fire is underrated," Smith growled. "It cleanses as often as it destroys. Those waters were international. They sent their planes buzzing around our heads, like gnats on a summer night. They got what was coming to them. They'd better wake the hell up and understand that we can, will, and *have* swatted them. They *will* learn this lesson, even if we have to shove it down their throats. The American military can't be attacked without significant reprisal."

"Well, what do you recommend?"

"We do not give the Chinese an inch!" Smith asserted. Then he stopped in his tracks, and Watkins awkwardly followed suit a brief moment later. Smith then turned so that he was looking his comrade in the eyes. "Listen, Watkins. Show the Chinese that the God-blessed United States of America does not back down from a fight."

United States National Security Advisor John Bannister blearily opened his eyes as the light of dawn filled his modest apartment. From the corner of his eye, he saw a woman rise from his bed, grab some crumpled bills on his bedside table, and walk away. By the time he heard his front door open and close, he rose from the bed, rubbed his hands over his cue bald head, and looked out his window. He smiled as he took in the comforting, if gray, sights of Washington, D.C. He saw his faint reflection in the window and took a moment to bask in self-satisfaction. At fifty-six years old, he looked better in boxer briefs than the vast majority of his fellow Americans.

His self-indulgence was interrupted by the loud ring of his cell phone, which came from his pants pocket on the side of his bed. After an enjoyable moment of recalling how his pants ended up there, he rushed to grab his phone.

Bannister had been expecting a very important call on this day.

"John Bannister," he affirmed.

"Hold for the president."

John nodded and waited patiently.

Eventually, a voice said, "John."

"I imagine peace talks are on the horizon."

"They are."

John frowned. "Mr. President, we can capitalize on this. We have been attacked by China. We suffered unthinkable casualties when *Austin* sunk. My god."

"What do you mean?" the president asked.

"The peace talks don't have to end in peace, if we don't want them to. We currently have a much stronger military than China, although they're catching up. We can fight now and settle this issue, while we still have a position of strength."

"Let's discuss this at the Emergency Cabinet Meeting."

FIVE
★ ★ ★
CHAPTER

B ill put a hand to his stomach. He chalked it up to nerves, but a part of him knew that was merely self-deception.

This could be the most pivotal peace talks I've ever participated in, he thought. *Mom, Dad, if you could see me now … I will make you proud.*

Memories of his parents brought back other thoughts about his family. *I loved growing up in Brooklyn, New York. It was a typical Irish neighborhood, and since both of my parents are Irish, we fit right in. Like so many others, their families had fled their homeland during the Potato Famine that devastated Ireland. Both sides of my family were part of the mass migration wave to America in the first half of the nineteenth century. Today, about ten percent of Americans are at least partly of Irish descent.*

Bill looked around his office. It was his home away from home. His sanctuary. *My grandfather would've made fun of me for this academic veneer*, Bill reminisced with a dry smile. *He was a rough guy. He was always bruised, tattered, or limping. His brutish face used to scare me as a kid. My grandfather had earned a living as a prizefighter. Back in the 1920s, Brooklyn was home to a lot of boxing clubs. They were major entertainment for men, as were Irish bars. It was illegal to sell liquor then, because of Prohibition. But there were still illegal bars, called speakeasies, on every corner in my neighborhood.*

Dad didn't take after my grandfather much. He was far more like his mother, who came from a more educated family than my grandfather. Dad was an excellent student growing up, eventually earning a scholarship to New York University. From what I'm told, he was very bookish as a teenager, but everything changed during his freshman year of college, when he was seventeen years old. The Japanese attack on Pearl Harbor really weighed on Dad. He and his friends decided to march for forty blocks and enlist in the army right then and there. Apparently, there was a five-hour line at the army's recruiting office in Times Square. I suppose they underestimated the patriotism that the Japanese attack would evoke in our red-blooded youth. They weren't ready for Dad and the legions of others ready to fight, so they just took down his name, address, and phone number.

Bill slowly walked against his cabinet of bookshelves, letting the familiarity of his collection of books comfort him. He slid a lazy finger across many of their spines. One of them caught his eye—an old book that his father had given him decades ago for his fifteenth birthday.

The book made Bill think of his father's life story. *Dad carried on with his collegiate career, waiting by the phone for the army to call. A couple of months later, they did. It turned out that he needed his parents' permission to join the army. My grandfather was fine with his decision, but my grandmother and great-grandmother didn't approve. My great-grandmother's opinion mattered, since she was like a mom to Dad while his real mom was always working. My father's always been a charmer, and after several weeks of begging and prodding, he earned everyone's approval.*

His basic training in the army lasted for six weeks. From what I'm told, he was a natural—strong-willed, capable, and quick on his feet. I like to think I inherited some of those qualities.

Dad told me that, one morning, he was ushered into a vast hall with over three thousand recruits, where they were all to take an aptitude test. Following the test, he was one of only three recruits selected from thousands to receive special training.

Tragically, many of my father's friends he finished boot camp with died at the hands of Germans led by Rommel. Dad's life was saved because he did well on a single test.

The army placed my father in a special unit whose purpose was to go behind enemy lines and report back everything they learned about the German enemy. As part of this unit, my father was sent to those most dangerous beaches on D-Day—June sixth, 1944. He was in the last wave of arrivals, and he fought all the way to Germany. Eventually he and his unit were caught behind enemy lines during the Battle of the Bulge, stuck with overwhelming German forces and tanks surrounding them.

They had learned that Nazis were executing soldiers that surrendered. This enraged them, and they became determined to fight until the end.

I would've been terrified if I had been in my father's shoes, but he was a natural warrior. He was one of the first Americans to cross into Germany at the Remagen Bridge, all the while under fire. Dad told me that there were people in his unit who were beginning to feel despondent about the battle, but they managed to capture the Ludendorff Bridge. The Germans tried to blow up the bridge, but many of their explosives failed to go off.

Dad did his job and reached the top of the hill, behind German lines. He radioed back their positions and level of strength. As he was marching to Berlin, he came across a strange camp with civilian prisoners. He realized that he had found a concentration camp. He shot open the locks on the gate and freed the prisoners, who looked like frail skeletons. He called his command, who sent medical support and food.

When Dad returned to America, he was rightfully treated as a war hero. He proposed on his first date with my mother, who said yes. He married her in short order, and I was born a few years after that. Back then, most veterans were quick to move on with their lives after the war. Maybe jumping right back into normalcy helped them adjust.

Dad volunteered to go to Korea when war broke out over there. He fought both the North Koreans and the Chinese with as much success as he enjoyed during World War II. This time, when he returned home, he ran for Congress and went on to serve for nearly thirty-five years. As a former soldier who saw friends and civilians die at war, he was a strong voice in the Senate against the war.

I fell in love with the lively political discussions that I'd have with Dad. And his district congressional office was only a few blocks away from our house, so I'd often go there and take it all in. I had so much fun helping my father with his reelection campaigns.

Once I went to college, I knew that I wanted to follow in Dad's footsteps and get into politics. He instilled in me a passion for understanding geopolitics, so naturally I majored in history at New York University.

Bill's eyes began to water, and the half-empty glass of beer became blurry. *I hope I've made you proud, Dad. I hope to make you proud.*

After a few minutes of mental wandering, Bill recalled many of the hostile, anti-American words he'd heard today from the Chinese. *How can they not see the good that America has brought to the world? The enemies of humanity that we have defeated? Hitler may have been far from China, but surely they can appreciate how we defeated the Japanese.*

And perhaps they don't like our involvement in the Korean War because they don't want us to impinge on their influence in the region. But I'm sorry, that's not an excuse for hating us. We and the rest of the Allies had just defeated Japan in World War II, which effectively ended over three decades of Japanese occupation of the Korean Peninsula. Korea was then split into a Soviet Union–occupied northern zone and a United States-occupied southern zone. We wanted the reunification negotiations to succeed. But communists are hardheaded ...

When North Korea invaded its southern counterpart in 1950, of course we had to defend our friends in South Korea. Over thirty-six thousand American heroes died defending South Korea. We were not the imperialists in the fight. We were defending the innocent.

Outside of Asia, we even helped Germany after World War II, despite Hitler's atrocities. We transformed their fascistic government into a liberal democracy. President Eisenhower led our policy of denazification. Our military went on to occupy the country and mandated that Germans fill out a questionnaire about their behavior during Hitler's reign. We categorized Germans as Major Offenders, Offenders, Lesser Offenders, Followers, and Exonerated Persons. We ended up with a list of about one-and-a-half-million veritable Nazis. I remember reading about the 1946 directive called "Removal from Office and from Positions of Responsibility of Nazis and Persons Hostile to Allied Purposes." We banned any Nazis from holding public office, which was crucial for the country's eventual democratization. Finally, on May eighth, 1949, the German Law was finalized. It was ratified on May twenty-third, and so the Federal Republic of Germany was born. We created the Marshall

Plan, through which we spent billions to rebuild Europe after the War. We included Germany in the plan.

And after we defeated Japan in World War II by forcing a surrender, they stopped occupying much of China. We turned them into a successful democracy, too.

Both Germany and Japan have been peaceful democracies ever since we helped them change their governments.

Maybe we failed in our messaging, that so many people think of Americans as imperialist warmongers. I don't know …

Bill's thoughts turned to China, where he knew that public opinion of America had seen better days. *The world will be watching us. Me and Yao, negotiating for peace. The Chinese may be on the rise, but America is not a country to be ignored. I can do this. For my father's honor, and his father before him, I will deliver peace.*

Because if I fail … so help me God … a war between our nations could destroy everything I love.

SIX
★★★
CHAPTER

"**T**hank you both," Yao said sincerely to the repairmen in his office.

Yao slowly paced around his office, careful to give the workers enough space to fix his desk before his team arrived.

"No problem, sir," one of the workers said. "How'd this happen, anyway?"

Yao smiled dryly. "It's an old desk. It was bound to happen sooner or later."

I never thought my vote against Bryers's desire to become secretary-general of the United Nations might come back to haunt me, Yao thought with concern. *It was the right decision, but ... I hope it does not complicate our peace talks. It's as if the universe is playing a joke on me.*

The foreign minister thought back to the retirement letter he knew that he could not send anytime soon. *If I cannot revive my wife, perhaps at least I can keep China's spirit alive. My father would have approved.*

In his fragile, sentimental state, Yao reminisced about what he knew about his father, Yao senior.

Father came from a lineage of prestigious military men and women. He was born in the military barracks, just west of Shanghai. In his day, each section of the city was controlled by Western colonial powers: America, Great Britain, and France.

I remember Father's stories about working as a deliveryman during college. With a basket of goods resting on the back seat of the bike, he'd cycle through the foreign enclaves in Shanghai. All of the colonists treated him with disrespect, and even the police would sometimes harass him and steal his deliverables. His boss, Samuel, was a British merchant who forced my father to pay him for anything that he failed to deliver.

The imperialists have always treated us as harshly as they could get away with. Even now, is that not what is happening in the South China Sea?

"Sir," one of the workers said, interrupting Yao's train of thought, "where would you like these documents?"

"Ah, please, place them on the right-hand side of the desk once it's back on its legs. Thank you."

The foreign minister smiled as he gazed at men far younger than he was fixing up his office. Their handiness brought back thoughts of his father.

Of course a man such as him could have attracted a woman as beautiful as my mother, Li. I've been told the story a dozen times. He was walking on the Bund, a waterfront in central Shanghai. The atmosphere is quite romantic—the main walkway hugs the western bank of the Huanggpu River on one side and skyscrapers on the other. Years later, in the 1970s and 1980s, government institutions on the Bund were replaced by financial powers. Then, in the 1990s, the Shanghai government worked to boost tourism in the district.

As Father was enjoying his evening stroll, he caught sight of a merchant ship coming into harbor. He told me that he saw a woman standing at the bow, and that he instinctively knew that she was beautiful. My father has always been a stoic, reserved man. But on that night, he mustered the courage to approach the woman. There was instant chemistry, and Father finished his walk with her by his side.

"Sir, would you like us to throw any of this away?" one of the workers asked, pointing to the remaining debris around the almost fully repaired desk.

"No, thank you. Better to keep that which I don't need than to throw away something important accidentally. Wouldn't you agree?"

The young man shrugged nervously. "Whatever you say, Foreign Minister. I keep my bills in my drawer at home."

Ah, to be so carefree, so young. I have the utmost respect for workers, as all good communists do. But how nice it must be to have such limited responsibilities. If I fail, billions of Chinese will suffer. The Americans have produced over 125,000 nuclear warheads since 1945, more than all other nations combined. The last estimate I read was that they harbored over six thousand nuclear warheads currently. We only have about three hundred and fifty. We have even pledged not to use nuclear weapons first in warfare. And yet, the West regards us as a threat. No matter what we do, they continue to imperialize.

Could we defeat the United States in all-out war? They've been so dominant for so many decades. But they have weaknesses that we can exploit. They are myopic, forgetful of the past …

Yao shook his head, eager to drop such unpleasant thoughts.

I remember Father telling me about his first few dates with my mother. After dinner one night, she showed him her bookshelves in her house. My mother pointed out The Communist Manifesto, *by Karl Marx. Apparently, it was her favorite book. My father requested to borrow it. I think that was the moment that they knew they were in love.*

The book changed Father's life. He knew, then, that he had to join Mao Zedong's communist movement. He told my mother of his intentions, and she was a little ambivalent. But then he proposed to her. She accepted, and he promised that he'd always prioritize her happiness over his political passions. With that, my father's plan to march was blessed by my mother.

I myself find Marx's work quite exhilarating. I've read all three volumes of his later work, Das Kapital. *When I came across his idea that capitalism includes the exploitation of workers to extract surplus value, I was floored. Of course that is the case! How could it possibly be otherwise? And yet the Americans have always balked at this idea. Marx had so many such ideas. And he is open-minded enough to give capitalism its due—capitalism* does *lead to technological improvement. But what the free market Westerners miss is that the same economic system that leads to better material conditions also leads to extreme inequality.*

Inspired by Marx, Father ended up participating in the Long March of 1934 to 1935, a military withdrawal of the Communist Party of China's Red Army. They were running from the Kuomintang Army, the Chinese Nationalist Party's forces. The Long March ushered Mao Zedong as the undisputed political power. He led my father and other communist supporters into safety, traveling nine thousand kilometers over the course of a year. This resulted in the relocation of the communist revolutionary base from southeastern to northwestern China.

Even before the Long March, Father was intimately involved with the Communist Red Army. He provided morale when the Chinese Soviet Republic was founded in Jiangxi in 1931, and he was loyal to Mao even as his standing fell during this time.

Father always lived by his principles, regardless of the pain or challenges that came his way. His military career allowed me to live a happy, innocent childhood for a while. When he was home, he'd teach me about everything—history, philosophy, proper etiquette, and how to thrive in this world. He inspired me to engage in politics from an early age, and I haven't looked back since.

Yao's eyes began to water, and he turned away so that the handymen could not see him. *My mother and I were so proud of him when he went off to fight in the Korean War. In late 1950, China entered the fray, and my father joined along with the rest of the People's Volunteer Army. I later learned how pivotal my father was in fortifying communication lines between North Korea's Kim Il Sung and Zhou Enlai, who by then was vice-chairman of the Central Military Committee.*

I remember when the gentleman knocked on our door, himself close to tears. He told us that Father was slain at the Battle of Onjong, where Chinese and American forces first clashed in Korea. I fell to my knees, utterly devastated.

But I knew that Father would've wanted me to continue working in service of China, so I did. Being the son of a war hero had its privileges, and I was fortunate enough to attend Beijing University on a stipend. I loved my time in school, and I fell in love with the city. Because of all of Father's history lessons, I had developed a passion for understanding the past. I studied history at college, and I'd visit the larger-than-life sites, like the Forbidden City and the Great Wall. I remember bringing my textbooks with me on my trips. I was almost literally reading about history while experiencing it at the same time.

"Hey, Foreign Minister," the other handyman said as he tested the table's robustness. "Everything in the papers, on television. Is it true?"

Yao turned back to the men. "It depends on what you've heard, doesn't it? Rest assured that we will handle the Americans. I promise you."

My beloved China. The United States is worried that we're becoming a superpower. But they don't appreciate our two-thousand-year history. I suppose from the West's perspective, we are just now rising onto the geopolitical scene. It's true that we were struggling politically, militarily, and economically in the nineteenth and early twentieth centuries. But this impoverished time period was an aberration. In the sixteenth century, Westerners were amazed at the riches we boasted. No, we are not an emerging *superpower. We are reemerging from a long and unfortunate slumber.*

How quickly the West forgets. For the first three centuries in which we engaged in steady contact with them, our leaders boasted mightier forces than theirs. Only when the British defeated the Qing Dynasty in the first Opium War of the nineteenth century did they finally gain the upper hand.

The West always brags about bringing the Industrial Revolution to the world in the eighteenth and nineteenth centuries, but we nearly beat them on the order of hundreds of years. And in the late fifteenth century, we were the core of a massive economic matrix, coordinating trade routes from South China to the Indian Ocean to the Red Sea. We are the civilization that invented printing, gunpowder, and the compass. We even had the first post office. At one point, we were so advanced that we cordoned ourselves off from the world because outsiders were all barbarians compared to us.

Ever since 1979, when we opened ourselves up to trade with the rest of the world, our GDP has grown nearly ten percent annually. Eight hundred million people have been lifted out of poverty since then. I'm proud that we are the globe's second-largest economy. We are the leading manufacturer and supply chain, and we own more foreign exchange reserves than any other nation.

I'm also proud of our government's more recent decisions. In the interest of continuing our growth, they've declared innovation to be one of their main focuses. I am confident in their 'Made in China 2025' plan, whose goal is to improve our manufacturing through government handouts. We'll become even less dependent on our Western trading partners. Good.

"Okay, Foreign Minister," one of the handymen said. "We're all finished. Is there anything else we can do for you?"

"That is all. May I ask, are you close with your families? Wives, girlfriends, perhaps?"

They nodded.

"Good. When you go home, please hug them. They may be worried over what they see on the news. China will survive this, and we will be stronger than ever. You may tell your family that Foreign Minster Sheng himself said so."

SEVEN
⎯ ★★★ ⎯
CHAPTER

Moscow, Russia

The pair of men walked between two rows of young workers, all of whom were hunched over their keyboards and staring at their large computer screens. They were all dressed in uniform—drab, baggy camouflage. Above the workers, televisions hung from the ceiling. They were broadcasting in English the twenty-four-hour news channel RT, which was a Russian state-owned and controlled international channel that expressed the Russian position on world issues. It was meant to counter CNN and BBC news.

"As you can see," Ivan said to the short but burly man walking beside him, "our team works around the clock, even at such a sleepy hour as this. They are still working twelve-hour shifts. We pay them well enough."

"Hold it for a moment," the other man said, and Ivan stopped in his tracks.

"Yes, Deputy Prime Minister Semenov?"

The politician eyed Ivan with a demeaning squint and a pouty lip. In his custom-fit, gray three-piece suit, Semenov gave the aura of someone who knew he was in charge. "This is the Internet Research Agency, yes? Well, let me see ..."

Semenov tapped a young, nerdish woman on the shoulder, who nearly jumped out of her chair. "Hello, ma'am," he said teasingly. "May I take a peek at your computer?"

She rose to her feet and bowed respectfully. "Mr. Semenov," she uttered nervously. "I had no idea you'd be here today."

"We did not want to distract you with such an announcement," Ivan explained.

"What's your name?" the politician asked.

"Anastasia."

"Anastasia, please, there is no need to stand for me," Semenov said. "Why don't you return to your computer and show me what you're doing?"

She nodded quickly. "Um, sure."

Semenov leaned over Anastasia's shoulder, his calm, steady breaths tickling her neck.

"Yes …" he whispered in near-ecstasy. "I know some programming myself. We old people can learn how to use computers, too. Your work looks sound." He pointed at one of the myriad windows of code on Anastasia's screen. "But please, save me some time. This looks like an algorithm. What is its purpose?"

"This automatically sets up a fake account on social media every twenty minutes," Anastasia answered, suddenly more confident. She pointed at a line of code towards the top of the particular window in question. "See this? Every morning when I come to the office, I toggle it to a different social media platform. So today, I'm sending bots to Twitter." She pointed at a timer on the bottom-left corner of her computer screen. "Another one will be born in four minutes, twenty-two seconds."

"I see," Semenov said approvingly. He then pointed to another window full of code. "This one is easier to read … you're ensuring that only Chinese and American names are used for your fake accounts. Do I have that right?"

"Uh, wow. Yes, exactly. Mr. Semenov, forgive me, but I didn't know that you were so well versed in coding. Most politicians are former military, intelligence officers, and some lawyers."

Semenov chuckled. "It's a different world now, miss. The military is not our greatest weapon. No, it's your keyboard, and your endless lines of code, and all of these wires, and"—he lightly tapped the top of Anastasia's head—"your mind. Anastasia, thank you for your time. You serve Russia honorably."

Anastasia's pale cheeks reddened, but her eyes lit up. "Thank you, sir."

The politician waltzed back to Ivan's side, and they continued walking.

"We have over two hundred people doing the same work as Anastasia is doing," Ivan said.

"I'm impressed, Ivan. You seem to run a smooth operation. The Kremlin will be pleased."

"Thank you, Mr. Semenov. To be frank, Anastasia is one of our newer coders. If you liked her work, you'll love what I have to show you after lunch."

Semenov nodded. "Tell me, what project most excites you that the coders are working on?"

Ivan placed a friendly hand on the politician's back. "They are currently figuring out how to coordinate not just individual bot accounts to manipulate Americans and Chinese on social media, but soon they will be creating entire pages and groups of bots. These clusters will be automatically populated by our bots, so they will appear to be very popular to anyone who comes across them. Then the bots will spread divisive misinformation on those pages. It will be a beautiful mess.

"The pages and groups are expected to have millions of followers. We already have the software in place to feed the groups information that is designed to prod Americans and Chinese into acting exactly as we want them to act. This works for the individual bots already. For example, we are responsible for leaking to the Americans that China is gearing up to attack their navy in the South China Sea. We did that precisely so that the Americans would be tempted to strike at China first, before they would become too strong. And look at what's happening on the waters. War could break out any day now."

"Very good, Ivan. This talk of psychological manipulation reminds me: I believe we are having dinner with the leading scientists from I.R.A. tonight, yes?"

Ivan nodded as the pair reached a door. He opened it, letting Semenov through first. They entered a quiet, empty hallway.

"Yes, that's right," Ivan answered. "Six of them, to be exact. Three sociologists and three psychologists. I've sat in on some of their lectures to the rest of the agency. They are some of Russia's greatest minds."

"It's more difficult to stir chaos on social media than one would think," Semenov said as they entered a fancy kitchenette. He began making a pot of coffee as he continued speaking. "Like most worthwhile pursuits, it is both an art and a science. I hope you don't mind, but I enjoy making my own coffee."

Ivan stood somewhat awkwardly against the kitchenette's refrigerator and shook his head in approval at the politician's actions. "From my own role as director, I have learned quite a bit about the human sciences. For example, our scientists have determined which words, phrases, and linguistic cues will spark outrage in both American and Chinese social media spheres. Interestingly, what works in one culture does not work in the other. Oh, and both cultures are constantly evolving, so our coders have developed algorithms to track changes regarding what works and what doesn't. They then lend the data to our scientists, who update their models." His thin lips spread from ear to ear. "The agency is a well-oiled machine, Mr. Semenov."

The politician put his hands in his pockets and stared at the coffee pot as it gradually filled. "How about the other departments?" he asked. "Any issues?"

"Our cybersecurity team is currently working on ways to exploit blockchain technology. This is a very new project, and I must admit that I don't fully understand it quite yet. There is an internal seminar about it next Tuesday, actually."

"Oh," Semenov said, still staring at the coffee pot. "Send me the recording, please. What about our bloggers? Any issues there?"

"No, none at all. As you know from your last visit, we are quite ruthless with our bloggers, as we must be. They are forbidden from making more than four mistakes per week, or else we fire them." Ivan chuckled. "Frankly, it has been an effective strategy for ensuring that we retain only the most talented writers. More businesses should act as we do."

"I don't think so," Semenov said. "This is covert intelligence work, not business. I have engaged in both, and I assure you that the rules of one do not carry over to the other. In any case, tell me the latest news about our law enforcement wing."

"Of course, sir. We recently hired another six law enforcement officers at the agency. That brings us to thirty-eight on staff. We only take in officers who have no relatives working here, by the way. It's a fairly new rule, so we've grandfathered in earlier hires. We did have to fire some people."

"I don't want to know, nor have the time to discuss, why you've implemented such a strange rule. Regardless, I still question their usefulness here."

"They monitor the unit and all of our employees' work and personal communication. This way, we stop any potential leaks of our activities to the press or to foreign spy agencies."

"Speaking of attention," Semenov said quietly, "I trust there are not any issues with our investigative journalists?"

"We vet them rigorously before allowing them here," Ivan answered. "They must be loyal Russians. What the world thinks it knows about the Internet Research Agency is mostly what we want them to know."

"Mostly," Semenov said ominously.

Ivan swallowed nervously. "There have been some slipups, I admit. The 2017 report by the United States intelligence community did not do us any favors. But we have added a number of security measures since then."

"What did they call the agency?" Semenov asked. He poured himself a cup of black coffee and finally turned back to face Ivan. "Ah, yes. A 'troll farm.' I've been in so many meetings about the report since then that I've practically memorized some of its passages. Thankfully, they projected America's politics onto our mission, which of course is a mere sliver of the truth. They were obsessed with the degree to which we influenced their last election. Self-centered fools, but it made our lives easier than if they'd kept digging."

Semenov took a step towards Ivan. "A year after the report was released, over a dozen Russian nationals were indicted by the United States, as was the agency. We cannot afford another such slipup."

"But since then," Ivan said quickly, "We have been feeding only information we want leaked to friendly international journalists. And our own internal journalists keep the Russian people complacent. You remember that Finnish journalist, Jessikka Aro, right? We made sure she was bombarded by harassment after she dared go after our people. Our defense mechanisms continue to improve."

After a lazy sip of his coffee, Semenov said, "I know. Ivan, the Internet Research Agency is less than ten years old. We have dealt many blows to our enemies, and we're still in our infancy stage. This operation is money well spent. I understand that there have been hiccups. But this could be the future—informational warfare, I mean. I'm truly impressed."

Ivan relaxed a little. "I'm glad to hear that, Mr. Semenov."

Semenov looked around to make sure they were alone. "Now, you know why I'm really here. I understand that we're in a secure location, but I didn't want to discuss your plans for tomorrow in front of any of your subordinates. Can't be too careful. Why don't you walk me through what will happen?"

"Sure. While we do have the ability to create artificial American and Chinese pages on social media, we are also able to infiltrate many huge political pages and groups with fake accounts. Our operatives behind the accounts have earned administrative status in many of these groups, and they hold sway over the other members. The activities have been in motion ever since the first debacle in the South China Sea occurred not long ago. Our operatives have arranged for rallies to break out tomorrow. Our coders have increased the number of likes and shares for favorable posts about the rallies. The time of the protests, the signs that should be carried, and even the tenor of the attendees have all been determined by our mass manipulation campaign. They will be bloodbaths."

"Good, Ivan. Need I bother asking if all sides of the political debate have been covered?"

Ivan smiled. "Of course, that has been taken care of. Not only will each country's citizens be at each others' throats, but the apathetic masses will have no idea what to believe. We've sprinkled falsehoods across all of the pages that are promoting the protests. Up is down, down is up."

The politician put his coffee down and gave Ivan's shoulder an intimidating, firm grip. "We have enjoyed many successes lately. We've affected elections in Nigeria and Ghana, tricked Americans into thinking that our fake websites are sincere American news sources, and even hacked into China's supposedly unassailable Internet infrastructure. I have a feeling that tomorrow will be an achievement for the history books."

Ivan was relieved at Semenov's change in outlook since he had first welcomed him to the building earlier that day. "I'm glad you think so, sir. In the end, China and the United States will tear each other apart. And Russia will be there to take the reins of power on the world stage."

EIGHT
★★★
CHAPTER

Washington, D.C.

B ill stood in the corner of the hallway outside his office, one hand holding his cell phone to his ear, the other on his hip.

"Yes, I know, kiddo," he said quietly. "But I have to do it."

"Just tell the president about your health," a loving voice said from the other end. "Can't they send someone else?"

"This is part of the job description, Michelle. It has to be me. There is no one else who will prevent a war."

Bill heard the woman lightly moan. "You need to slow down, Dad. We want you around. We love you."

"I know, I know. I love you t—" Bill winced and grabbed his stomach in pain.

"Dad? Are you alright?"

"Yeah," he answered quickly. "I'm fine. Everything's fine."

"Do you know when you're leaving? How long will you be gone?"

Bill shook his head. "I'm leaving later today but I don't know for how long. When I find out, you'll be the first to know. Hey, I have to go meet the rest of the team now. The ones who are coming with me."

"I love you, Dad. Please stay safe."

"I will. I love you, too."

Bill placed his phone in his pocket and headed down the hall, stopping in front of a vanilla office door. Before he turned the doorknob, he brought his ear close to the door. He smiled at the sounds of energetic chatter. Only then did he open the door.

The office was small, with a few computers by the walls and a single, long table in the center. Two men and a woman sat at the table, all in their late thirties to early forties. As Bill closed the door behind him, the room fell silent, and the secretary of state felt the focus of dozens of pairs of eyes on him.

"Hello," Bill said with open, friendly arms. "My name is Bill Bryers, but please just call me Bill. You've all been picked as my staff in our upcoming talks with China."

One of the men, Josh, had worked with Bill for years. He was wiry, freckled, and had a nose that looked as if it had been broken once or twice.

After the others nodded, Bill approached them. Bill looked over each of them with careful scrutiny. His eyes settled on two diplomats who were sitting in the front. Sara was small, with mousy black hair and features so slight and angular that she could have been a model from the nineties. Thomas was broad-shouldered and dark-eyed but held a friendly disposition that offset his intimidating appearance.

"As you already know, Josh has been promoted to assistant secretary of state," Bill announced.

"Yes, sir," uttered many diplomats.

"Good. I've heard positive things about all of you." He pointed at Sara. "Are you ready for what's to come?"

"I've worked in international relations for a while," Sara answered.

"This situation is beyond volatile. Please know that I don't exaggerate. We are on the brink of a world war, and this is maybe our only shot at avoiding it. One mistake could cost us, our country, and quite literally the fate of humanity."

"No pressure," Sara joked nervously.

"Thomas," Bill said, "what do you think?"

"From my experience, the proceedings could be very mundane, despite the enormous consequences," Thomas said.

Bill nodded. "Long, boring talks are the best we can hope for. In this case, we'd better hope that nothing exciting happens. With skill and some luck, we'll shake hands with the Chinese, reconcile, and be on our way."

"Have you spoken to them yet?" Sara asked.

"I spoke with their foreign minister, Yao Sheng. He's a real son of a bitch. Arrogant. Implacable. We'll have to break through to him, somehow. I've negotiated with him before. It didn't end well."

"We got this," Thomas said, grinning from ear to ear.

"I'm glad you're confident," Bill said. "Sources tell us that Russia has already agreed to back China in the event of violent conflict. We need to show Sheng that we're willing to go the extra mile to keep an open dialogue between our nations."

"We're flying to the other side of the world!" Thomas said between chuckles. "That's not enough?"

"It's a start," Bill answered sternly. He turned to Sara. "I'm told you speak fluent Chinese."

Sara nodded and suddenly sat upright. "That's right. Mandarin, to be precise."

Bill was relieved at her surge of confidence. *She seemed nervous at first. Better that we all exude certainty for as long as we can. The Chinese won't respect any signs of weakness.*

Josh reentered the room and took his seat at the table. He looked up at Bill and asked, "What did I miss?"

"Nothing," Bill answered. "Just making sure everyone's on the same page. I'm told that the Chinese will be receiving us with open arms, fine accommodations, and the like."

Josh scoffed. "They are always good hosts. It's tradition."

People began to speak amongst each other, as the formality of Bill's meeting dissipated.

"Josh," Sara said in an annoyed tone, "we're lucky they're even willing to meet with us after what happened! America and China are the two superpowers of the world. We have to learn how to keep the peace and work together."

"Sara's right," Bill said, ignoring the background chatter of everyone else. "We need to focus on improving our relations. The key is to find common ground."

"I like Peking duck," Thomas said. "Does that count?"

The four of them shared a laugh. After a few moments, Bill put his hands out and brought everyone in the room's attention back on him. "Okay, okay. Thanks for that, Thomas. So we have at least one thing in common with the Chinese. Now, let's focus. We have a lot of work ahead of us. I haven't actually seen Sheng in over two decades. Who knows—maybe he'll be easier to work with this time around. We'll need to think carefully about how to establish a trustful relationship with him."

"Maybe you can tell him that you're sorry about his wife," Sara said. "She recently passed away."

Bill blinked but kept his cheerful expression. "Thank you, Sara. It will be tricky business, since, while our men shot first, they fought back with unnecessary aggression."

"What if we let them expand their territory in the South China Sea?" Sara asked.

Bill pursed his lips. "Maybe. On the other hand, that may prompt them to expand their territory even further. We'd be feeding the beast."

"What if we offered them nothing?" someone in the back shouted.

Bill shook his head. "That's unlikely to help us achieve peace. We'll have to meet them in the middle, somehow. Anyway, we don't need to solve this issue now. I just wanted to bring it up so that it's in all of your minds. But in any case, let's go. We can get to know each other on the plane ride over to Beijing. Gather your belongings and meet me at the front desk in half an hour. Air Force Two is being made available for the trip."

"The president's backup plane," someone said. "Impressive."

Josh stood against a stony column in a dark, empty parking garage. His black hood covered most of his face, and the area's shadows covered the rest. He turned his head as a sedan came rolling by, until he was inches from the driver's window.

The window slid down to reveal National Security Advisor John Bannister's bald head. He nodded at Josh. "Where'd you tell Bill you were going?"

Josh smiled. "Told him I had to make a quick phone call. He trusts me, John. I could've said anything."

"Well, if that doesn't put my faith in our God-blessed institutions, I don't know what would."

"You got what you came here to give me?" Josh asked.

"Here." John threw a bulky manila envelope towards Josh.

Josh opened the envelope to find a digital Dictaphone, a small black sphere, and a tiny bottle.

"Get our friend Bill talking smack about the Chinese foreign minister," John said. "That Dictaphone, make sure you know how to use it. Record Bill. We'll take care of the rest."

Josh shook his head. "You think this is enough? We need to turn the tide, not just give them a black eye, Bannister."

"Once you destroy the last appearance of trust, the missiles will start flying ... then we can crush China."

"What's the bottle for?"

"In case of any ... obstacles. I'll tell you about it later, so you're not tempted to use it too soon."

"Got it. Fine, then. You will have no customs since you have a diplomatic passport."

John gave Josh one last smile. "Have a safe flight. Don't lose your luggage."

NINE
★★★
CHAPTER

Bill and the rest of the diplomats stood outside the front of the State Department as Bill's limousine arrived.

"Secretary Bryers?" a gruff voice said from afar.

Bill turned to see Admiral Smith approaching him. He smiled and shook the admiral's hand. "Admiral! What are you doing in my neck of the woods?"

Smith shook his head. "Still hard to believe you're not a senator anymore. Anyway, the national security advisor set up a briefing with the other Joint Chiefs on the South China Sea conflict. Seems like it could be at the tipping point of becoming a full-blown war."

Bill instinctively felt the attention of the other diplomats on him, but he ignored them. "Hopefully you can convince the Chinese that this is nothing more than a case of human error on our end."

Smith clenched his jaw. "Well, hold on now. It takes two to tango. They may need to learn a lesson. Either way, you know I'll be there."

Bill frowned. "Admiral, respectfully, lives are on the line. Let's give diplomacy a chance."

The admiral nodded. "I'm flying out tomorrow. I'll see you there."

As the driver began placing their luggage in the back of the limousine, Bill saw another man approach Admiral Smith, whom he recognized as John Bannister.

"Admiral Smith," Bannister said as they shook hands. "Glad you could make it for the briefing."

"Of course. Admittedly, I'm more interested in your off-the-record comments than anything else, though."

Bannister paused and watched the limousine take the secretary of state and the other diplomat away. Once it was out of sight, he turned his eyes back to Smith and whispered, "The president likes to talk a tough game, but even he still wants to stay on good terms with the Chinese. We need to show him that if we don't fight now, in a decade they'll be able to militarily dominate us."

Smith leaned in a little closer. "What about these peace negotiations?"

"Our nation's future depends on their failure."

They stepped away from each other but held eye contact. No more words were needed. They understood what had to be done.

Beijing

Yao Sheng sat at his office desk, eager to host his team of several dozen diplomats.

It was a very crowded room. Most of the diplomats were in their thirties or forties—with some notable exceptions—and were all standing and looking at Yao with professional deference.

"Thank you all for coming," Yao said after brief introductions were made. "The American diplomats arrive today. Let's do everything we can to ensure that their visit is comfortable and tolerable. We—"

"Do you anticipate a quick visit?" a man in the front, Chen, interrupted with a grin.

Yao frowned at Chen, who immediately dropped his smile. "Chen, you're smart, and charming. But remember that I am your superior. Interrupt me again and I will find a replacement."

Chen nodded and cast his big eyes to the floor in embarrassment. "Yes, sir."

"Guo," Yao said, turning to the female assistant. "You have the most expertise in American history and culture. I need you to interpret the American's intentions."

Guo had the build of an athlete and wore no makeup or jewelry. She nodded. "Quite confident. I spent enough time in the States to get their quirks, sayings, and habits."

"Excellent," Yao said. Then he turned to Huang, a chubby man with stubble that he did not seem to tend to. He looked a bit older than Chen and Guo. "Huang, you've spent many years as a diplomat in the United States. Do you have any advice?"

"Indeed," Huang answered. "Never lose control of your emotions. One undisciplined outbreak could ruin the entire negotiations. They will be typical Americans and try to cut a quick deal. We need to use this opportunity for them to acknowledge our territories in the seas."

Yao nodded. "I realize that the issues on the table will be challenging to discuss with the Americans. Disagreement is inevitable. With the escalating events in the South China Sea, it is understandable for you to be apprehensive, or outright distrustful of the Americans." Yao raised his hands and made fists for the other diplomats to see. "But we must not allow war to erupt. Miscommunications will happen, but they need to be corrected whenever they emerge. We must maintain dialogue with the Americans."

Guo replied, in English, "Sir, with respect, I know what you're really saying. The Americans think that everyone has to cater to them, to speak their language."

Yao sighed but conceded the point with a gesture. "I'm not looking forward to negotiating with their secretary of state, Bill Bryers. I've worked with him in the past. He's condescending and bound to hold a grudge against me. Years ago, I opposed his nomination to secretary-general of the United Nations. Still, it is vital that we show our hospitality to our foreign counterparts. Let's show the world our willingness to work with the Americans. The eyes of many peoples will be upon us."

"And history will remember this summit," Huang said softly.

Beijing Airport

The crowd of Chinese diplomats stood with a dozen other Chinese officials, as they all awaited the Americans. Yao saw a man approaching him from the corner of his eye.

"Commander Wong," Yao said. "I did not expect you to join us here."

"Many of our brethren in the military are quite concerned about your summit. They think it's reckless."

Yao kept his expression stoic, guarding against his emotions. "*They* do, or you do?"

"There are questions over whether you should even be inviting a diplomatic delegation from a country that has trespassed in *our* waters and fired upon *our* aircraft," Wong replied hotly.

Your tone answers my question, Yao thought. "The peace talks are happening," he said flatly.

Wong scrunched his eyebrows aggressively. "The Americans must see that we won't be bullied. We fought them in the Korean War, and we are ready to stand up to them again."

Yao stared at Wong for an extended moment, then put a hand over his heart. "You know that the Americans killed my father in Korea. Don't play that card."

"They're here!" one Chinese official said loudly.

Yao and Wong turned their heads to see the several dozen Americans emerge from the terminal. Yao quickly turned back to Wong and whispered, "Don't you dare undermine this."

As the Americans approached them, Yao walked over to Bill and extended a hand. "Welcome to China, Secretary Bryers."

Bill took Yao's hand and said, "Thank you."

Yao nodded. "Of course. How was your flight?"

"Easy. It'll take some time to adjust to the time difference, I'm afraid, but I'm glad we're all here."

"Last time we met," Yao said, trying to be friendly, "you were a senator and chairman of Foreign Relations."

Bill's expression flashed in anger for a moment, but then he smiled forcibly. "Yes, well, things change. Thank you for the invitation, Minister."

Josh, Sara, and Thomas shook hands with Chen, Guo, and Huang in stiff, frosty exchanges.

"We have a limousine waiting for all of us," Yao said to Bill. "Please, come this way."

"Where are we headed?" Bill asked.

"We have arranged a welcome banquet for you, as our guests of honor."

Bill nodded. "Right. Okay, I know everyone's hungry."

As the large group headed towards the airport's exit, Yao asked Bill, "Have you ever been to the Forbidden City banquet hall?"

"No, I haven't," Bill answered curtly.

After an awkward pause, Yao sensed the tension and said, "Secretary. I was hoping that we could set our past differences aside. For the sake of all of us."

Bill tilted his head and looked at Yao with utter apathy. "I don't forgive you, Minister. Don't be ridiculous. But I'm here to do my job. So I urge you not to mention it."

Yao pursed his lips and did not respond. *I tried*, he thought to himself. *But there is hope yet. Nothing eases tension like a warm meal. I think an immediate banquet will have turned out to be a wise decision. Everything will be fine.*

Even in his own mind, Yao could hear the worry in his words.

TEN

★ ★ ★

CHAPTER

Rural Michigan

A group of unshaven white men in army fatigues stood within a cluster of trees, where no one could see them. Each carried a different type of automatic weapon, and each boasted a Nazi tattoo of a swastika.

"Now is the time to strike," Joe said after he spat on the ground. "All these commie-loving liberals are going to protest against war. They want to protect China. Utter fools."

"Finally," Joe's brother, John, said anxiously. "I've been waiting for a call to action. Let's put our two new volunteers on the ground. They'll do anything we ask, and they'll blend well into the crowd. They look like vegan commies."

The men laughed at that.

"Where are they now?" Joe asked impatiently.

"In Chicago," John answered. "They're practicing throwing grenades. They're husband and wife, too, which always lowers people's suspicions."

Joe smiled. "Good. Let's see what they can do."

Seven Hours Later

Chicago, Illinois

Mike and Jane stood watching the crowd marching through the streets of their city. They were dressed in all black, which conveniently concealed their aggressive tattoos. Mike was tall, bald, and muscular, while Jane was a shade too thin, wore her black hair in a bun, and stood nearly a foot shorter than Mike.

"It's disgusting," Mike muttered. "Chanting 'peace with China, say NO to war.' Look at all of these reporters, sympathetically interviewing protesters in the streets."

Jane grabbed his hand lovingly.

"You know what we have to do," Mike said quietly.

Jane nodded submissively.

The couple stood at a street corner, wearing baggy jackets to hide their belongings.

"Look, another pig," Mike said, pointing at a police officer who strolled into the scene. "I'd say we're ready."

The two of them looked at each other one last time.

And then they both pulled grenades out from their jackets and threw them into the crowd.

A loud explosion went off. Mike and Jane watched as men, women, and children cried in terror as people lay in the street, dead or severely injured. The crowd ran for safety.

The sound of automatic weapons rang from a nearby rooftop, followed by more screams.

"Come on!" Mike yelled, gripping Jane's hand more firmly as they practically dove into the crowd.

Gunshots went off all around them, followed by more screams and cries.

Mike smelled blood, and it made him smile. Then he pulled out the kitchen knife from his jacket pocket.

"Communists, die!" he yelled madly as he stabbed the nearest body he could find.

A Chicago SWAT team quickly arrived at the scene and immediately began returning fire at the white supremacists who were shooting at the crowd from the rooftop. One of the terrorists was struck in the chest, and the policemen encircled the rooftop in case another of the shooters stuck his head out.

"Mike, let's get out of here!" Jane said.

"Just keep holding my hand!" Mike shouted. "Our friends will hide us!"

The duo ran along with the chaotic crowd, while policemen frantically tried to keep the peace. After a few minutes, the couple reached the next block.

At the end of the block, a man stood on a simple cardboard box, holding a microphone.

"You see what those neo-Nazis do?" the protestor cried. "Don't let them stop us! Find them and kill them!"

Three policemen charged the man, tackled him, and handcuffed him.

"Hey, I saw you throw the grenades!" a grating voice said from within the crowd. "Get them!"

Mike could feel Jane's hand shaking inside his as the crowd surrounded them.

The crowd started to kick and hit the pair as they were pushed to the ground. Just as Mike was reaching for another grenade, two of the policemen broke through the crowd.

"Help us!" Jane begged the policemen.

The police looked at each other and then pointed their weapons at the crowd.

"Everyone, stand down!" one of them announced.

"Arrest them!" one of the marchers shouted back.

Mike tore his hand away from Jane's and put them up in the air. "Okay, okay, it was me! Arrest me, officer, not her!"

The crowd began to chant: *"Arrest him, arrest him!"*

Just as one of the policemen readied to put Mike in handcuffs, Mike managed to pull out a grenade. The other police officer from the pair backed away, fearing what Mike would do. Mike saw that Jane was already in handcuffs and being dragged to a police car, so he darted away into the nearest alley.

He quickly reached the alley and surreptitiously dashed into one of its hidden doors.

Inside, a few men and women stood around, cleaning their guns and smoking cigarettes.

"Well?" the oldest man asked.

Mike nodded. "Part One is complete."

"What about my sister?" a skinny woman dressed in a motorcycle outfit demanded.

"They ain't gonna harm her," Mike asserted confidently.

Mike pointed towards the guns on the only table in the dilapidated shell of a former bar. "Are those ready?"

"Yeah," someone said.

Mike calmly walked over, grabbed a small gun, and tucked it into his pants. "Good. Time for Part Two."

The rest of them continued to ask Mike questions, but all he heard was white noise.

He returned to the alleyway but ran further down it, towards the other street, away from the march.

Jane, God, please be okay, he thought anxiously.

Mike found a nearby café and slipped into a chair in their outdoor seating area. He watched the street with care.

Four cop cars, one at each corner. March should pass through here in a few minutes.

"Hello, sir," a waitress said in a soft voice. "Drink to get you started?"

Mike nodded without taking his eyes off the scene. "A coffee, please."

Trying to make small talk, the waitress said, "Crazy, isn't it? I see so much strife on Twitter and Facebook about the South China Sea, and now it's come to life here in Chicago."

"These communist sympathizers want China to control the world."

Before the waitress could answer, two people on motorcycles entered the street, blasting past the police cars at ninety miles per hour. They came to a screeching halt at the street's halfway point.

Mike smiled. *Welcome to the party, friends.*

Two policemen exited their car and pointed their guns at the bikers. "Stop or we will shoot! Put your hands up!"

One of the motorcyclists took a gun out of his jacket and shot at the policemen. The police took cover behind their car. Backup police arrived, left their cars, and began to fire back. Gunfire struck one of the motorcyclists, who fell to the ground immediately with a scream of pain.

Just as the gunfight broke out, the anti-war march entered the street from the other side.

One of the motorcyclists revved his engine and drove straight towards the marchers. Policemen struck him down with gunfire before he managed to reach the crowd.

With that, Mike jumped to his feet, knocking over his chair in the process. He pulled out his gun and began firing on the policemen, laughing the whole time.

"Oh my god!" the waitress breathed in a panicked tone as she ran back inside the café.

Police tried shouting orders, but the scene was too chaotic for anyone to understand anyone else.

A bullet shattered the café's window. Mike looked at the police, who had turned their attention towards him.

He gave one last look at the motorcyclists, bleeding on the ground, who stood in stark opposition to the mob.

We will remember your sacrifice, Mike thought. *The few against the many. The righteous against the enemy. When we take control of this country, you will become national heroes.*

One of the policemen marched towards Mike, his gun raised, ready to fire. "Put the gun down and get on your knees!"

Mike heeded the command, keeping his eyes on his dying friends.

As Mike's knees touched concrete, he smiled.

Tiananmen Square, Beijing, China

Two hours after dawn broke, thousands of buses dropped protesters off at the enormous, famous square. They organized themselves across the white bridges that led to the massive red building before them.

The entire process was extremely well organized. As protesters left the buses, others stood ready to hand them signs and direct them.

The signs read, in both English and Chinese, "Stop the imperialist Americans," "Go home America's Navy," and "The South China Sea is ours."

Television crews from all over the world were covering this historic protest.

"Alex," a British news anchor said to a reporter on the ground via video, "this crowd is absolutely staggering. Care to guess how many people are at Tiananmen Square?"

"I'm told about three hundred thousand, Steve. But I'm also told that the buses are still coming. One analysis predicts over one million protesters by the end of the day."

"What do you think this means?" Steve asked.

"Well, this is clearly organized by the Chinese government. It is a sign that they are not willing to back down against the power that is the United States. Participants in this protest have told me that they are well aware that the United States' and China's navies are on a collision path to war."

Steve frowned. "Not a good sign, Alex. Please stay safe over there."

"I will, Steve."

ELEVEN
★ ★ ★
CHAPTER

Beautiful artwork covered the walls of the Forbidden City's banquet hall. Statues of dragons, paintings of people from another era, golden lanterns, and esoteric imagery surrounded the American diplomats. As Bill took his seat at the dining table and looked around the room, an unsettling feeling swept over him.

Chinese calligraphy is everywhere, he noticed. *That golden dragon with five claws on each foot is the symbol of the emperor. During some Chinese dynasties, the white dragon portended death as a warning.* He laughed when he noticed an American flag pinned above the doorway, adjacent to the Chinese flag. He turned his head to the other side of the hall, where performers were dancing in traditional costumes, accompanied by Chinese music.

The American diplomats sat on one side of a large, round table, while their Chinese counterparts sat on the other side. The music and entertainment sideshow prevented the silence between the two parties from feeling too awkward.

As Bill's attention was on the show, a performer entered the stage in a long, trailing dragon costume. She—the performer had a feminine physique, from what Bill could see—moved the dragon about using white poles. Suddenly and fiercely, the dragon's jaws snapped open and shut in the direction of the diplomats. The performers then bowed and left the stage, although the music still played.

Bill tapped his foot anxiously and glanced quickly to his American partners, doing his best to communicate solidarity through facial expression alone.

Servers in pink dresses quietly delivered plates of impeccably arranged food to the center of the diplomats' table. The food was arranged in a large, lazy Susan style. The turntable was clearly intended to be rotated as people desired different food items. Steam from the dishes filled Bill's eyes as the waiters removed their coverings. He saw dumplings, lobster, noodles, and a few dishes he could not place. Two types of soups were placed next to each plate, each in a beautiful Chinese bowl that was decorated with red and gold dragons. Bill's stomach growled, but he knew better than to dive in.

"Everyone," Yao announced, "I look forward to our upcoming talks. But tonight, let us enjoy life. I believe the English word for this is *leisure*." He gestured towards the dishes. "We Chinese are famous for our hospitality towards our guests. Please, let us know if there is anything we can do to make you more comfortable. Now, I insist, help yourself."

The American diplomats exchanged looks one more time. Thomas shrugged and muttered, "Yao says so." He took the server's spoon in the bowl of noodles and carefully placed more than one serving onto Bill's plate. The rest of the Americans followed suit in serving themselves. Only after that did the Chinese diplomats help themselves.

"Mmm," Thomas, who was sitting next to Bill, noised as he ate. Bill eyed him, but Thomas only responded with an apologetic shrug.

Even as they ate, Bill sensed both awkwardness and tension. Few words were spoken, save for a request for passing along a particular dish. Anytime he would look at the Chinese, he noticed how stiff they seemed.

So professional as to be completely bland, he thought.

"Minister … I was sorry to hear about your wife," Bill said.

Suddenly, all eyes were on Yao. He looked down, avoiding all eye contact. "Thank you," he said quietly.

Sensing the awkwardness, Bill said, "What I mean is, my sincere condolences for your—

He stopped himself as Yao looked up at him with an icy gaze.

New dishes kept coming to the table as the old ones were removed. With each new dish, Yao explained what it was and from which part of China it originated.

After countless dishes, the music faded, and the diplomats were left sitting at the table with stuffed bellies and nothing to say.

"This was delicious," Sara said politely. "Thank you all."

Yao and his diplomats nodded in appreciation. "I hope it was to your satisfaction."

Thomas wiped his mouth after a final bite, having eaten more than anyone else at the table. "Definitely!"

"You will have a great view of the Great Wall on the way to our hotel," Yao said.

"I think we'd like that," Josh said. "What's the plan?"

Yao rose from his seat. "Come, there is a limousine awaiting us."

As they drove away, a convoy of almost thirty vehicles—limousines, cars, military vehicles, and a bus of reporters—followed them.

It took nearly an hour to reach the Great Wall. Bill struggled to not drop his jaw as he stared at the stunning edifice through the car window. Although he had seen it before, the structure still amazed him. Even unadorned, the structure radiated ancient power that poured over him. "That is really something," he muttered to himself.

"Something to admire, isn't it?" Yao said.

Bill turned to Yao, who was sitting next to him in the limousine. He smiled at his Chinese counterpart, relieved that they could talk about something outside of politics. "It's stood the test of time more than most creations of man. That alone is worth appreciating. Add to that the role it's played in history, and yeah—it's worthy of admiration."

Yao nodded proudly. "Twenty-three hundred years old. Thirteen thousand miles long. It was initially built to separate three warring states. Later, the walls were extended and unified by Emperor Qin in order to secure China's border."

"The Chinese have always been protective of themselves," Bill noted. "So are the Americans, I assure you."

"This wall kept out many foreign invasions, until the Europeans came by ship and colonized our land. We have historic reason to distrust foreigners."

"How territorial of you," Bill said.

Yao looked back at Bill, his expression stonelike. "Indeed. What you Americans claim in the South China Sea is thousands of miles from your country. If we had a naval fleet two hundred miles from San Francisco, would you not panic?"

Bill shook his head. "Apples and oranges, Yao."

Yao put his hands up and sat back, signaling that the conversation was over.

Some time later, Bill looked out the window to see the gorgeous rural wilderness of the Chinese countryside. He noticed some signs, but they were all written in Chinese characters. Light snow peppered the ground and the tree leaves. As the limousine continued onwards, a sprawling lodge entered Bill's view. Behind the lodge was a backdrop of majestic mountains and the Great Wall itself.

"We have arrived," Yao announced.

As the diplomats entered the lodge's lobby, Bill noticed the golden statues, lamps, and chandeliers that decorated the otherwise wooden scene.

It's practically more gold than wood in here, he thought.

"Aside from maintenance staff," Yao told the group as a pair of well-dressed gentlemen took their bags, "we have the entire lodge to ourselves. We will have the space and privacy required for our discussion."

"What about security?" Thomas asked.

Yao nodded. "Precautions have been taken. We are safer here than almost anywhere else in the entire country."

"I'll take your word for it," Thomas replied.

"You've all had a long journey," Yao said, looking at the Americans. "I'm guessing you'll want to retire for the evening, so that you're well rested for tomorrow's talks."

Bill looked at his watch but laughed when he realized that, although he was very far from home, he did not need to adjust his watch. Beijing was exactly twelve hours ahead of Washington, D.C. He looked up at Yao and said, "Yes, that sounds good."

Yao nodded. "Follow me to the elevators."

As the group approached the elevators, Yao pressed a button and gestured for the Americans to enter.

"Are you coming up as well?" Bill asked.

"We're staying in the east wing, which is in the other direction." Yao grinned. "I assumed that you would be most comfortable in the west wing."

The Americans who entered the first elevator with Bill all chuckled. "Of course," Bill replied.

"Good night, thanks again for your generous hospitality," Sara said.

"The pleasure was ours," answered Guo. "See you tomorrow."

The elevator doors shut. Bill closed his tired eyes and let out a sigh of relief. The security detail in the elevator quietly signaled for everyone to be quiet. He then pulled out an apparatus to check for listening devices. After a few seconds, he signaled that all was clear.

"That wasn't so bad," Thomas said cheerfully.

"That was the easy part," Bill muttered.

"Thomas, please," Josh said. "That couldn't have been more awkward. Hey, Bill, you and Yao sure seem like you know each other well."

"Yeah, like I said, we have been adversaries many times." Bill paused and continued, "If it wasn't for Yao's veto, I'd be secretary-general of the UN right now, enjoying my time at the UN."

The elevator halted with a *ping!* and the doors opened. Bill exited first, and the others quietly followed their leader.

Some of the Chinese diplomats sat in a circle of couches in the lounge room on the first floor. Others remained standing, since there were not enough couch seats for all of them.

"All through dinner, you could have cut the tension in the air with a butter knife," Huang grumbled.

"Did you see their poker faces when they got in the limousine?" Chen added. "They're here to play hardball."

"I expect so," Guo offered. "The secretary can act all nice, and then stick a knife in your back."

"Something you all should know," Yao said. "When Mr. Bryers was a senator, he was very anti-China. I can't say I trust him."

"We shouldn't trust any of them," Chen said.

Yao pursed his lips. "Americans are used to getting what they want, playing by rules that they've established. We need to stand our ground. This summit has to be a success for us. We want the United States and the rest of the world to recognize our legitimate rights in the South China Sea."

"We'll smile for them," Guo said, offering a mocking grin. "Put on a good show, play nice."

Yao nodded. "Let's find some issues to agree upon, then send them on their way. And with their goddamn navy."

In his impressively spacious lodge room, Bill took off his tie and unbuttoned his shirt in front of the bathroom mirror. With no hands, he held a satellite phone to his ear.

"Did I wake you?" he asked gently.

"No, not at all!" said a female voice from the other end.

"Good, good. You guys have breakfast yet?"

The woman answered, but static distorted her words.

"I'm sorry, kiddo, I can't hear you. The line's bad. One sec."

Bill finished taking his shirt and tie off and walked towards the center of his bedroom, hoping to find a better signal. "Hello?"

"Dad? Can you hear me? Any word on my husband?"

"Ah, much better. No, not yet. They are still looking for survivors. Don't give up hope."

"Okay, okay. Well, how is it over there? How are you?"

Bill rubbed his eyes and looked around his room. It was well appointed but rather stark. "Things are as good as I could expect them to be. And I'm fine, a little stressed."

"Stay strong like I know you will. I miss you."

Bill's eyes welled up. "I'll be back before you know it. Kiss the girls for me. I love you."

"You, too."

Bill hung up and put the phone down on a table below the room's television. He took out a special, secure satellite phone and made another call.

After brief formalities, Bill said, "Mr. President, we start our formal talks tomorrow."

The president gave stark orders.

"Yes, sir," Bill answered seriously. "I will take a hard stand on our use of the South China Sea for our navy. Goodbye."

As Bill hung up, he frowned and grabbed his stomach in pain. The secretary of state walked over to his luggage bag, unzipped a small pocket on its side, and pulled out a plastic bag with several bottles inside. He returned to the bathroom, opened the bag, and grabbed the first bottle that he touched. He read the words on its label: "PATIENT: WILLIAM M. BRYERS."

Yao leaned over the sink in his lodge room's bathroom and splashed water over his face. When he looked up into the mirror, he eyed the golden wedding ring on the bathroom counter. After drying his face, he slipped the ring back onto his finger.

I'm sorry, he thought, visualizing his family. *For China, I must do this. And I will succeed.*

TWELVE
★★★
CHAPTER

South China Sea

U nderwater in a Virginia-class submarine, communications officer Ryan handed a classified cable marked 'urgent' to the captain.

The captain nodded silently and read the words on the cable: 'This is not a drill. Go immediately to these coordinates at the bottom of the sea and stay there with the engines off. Go radio silent. At the top of each hour, check for communications. Prepare to launch cruise missiles at the following targets …'

The executive officer took the cable from the captain and read the words on it as well.

"My god," he breathed. "We're hitting China."

"We have orders," the captain asserted.

Summit Lodge, China

The American diplomats were escorted to a large, barren auditorium by one of the lodge's workers. In the early morning, they shuffled in and sat in the staggered rows of chairs facing the pulpit at the front of the room. At the back of the auditorium, a U.S. security detail was sweeping the room to check for listening devices.

Bill held in his yawn as he and a younger colleague, Darren, took to the podium.

Once everyone had settled in, Bill raised a hand, and everyone turned to him. The secretary of state adjusted the podium's microphone and said, "Good morning, colleagues. As you know, our negotiations with the Chinese are rapidly approaching—in a few hours, we will meet with them in another room. For now, though, I want to ensure that we all understand Chinese culture and history. If we engage with them without this knowledge, we could guarantee failure. With that, I'd like to give the podium to Darren Stapleton, one of our aides and an expert on Chinese history and culture."

Bill took a few steps back, and Darren took his place. "Thank you, Mr. Secretary. Please, everyone, treat this meeting as an informal conversation. Raise your hand at any point, and I would be happy to answer your questions. I know some of you are Chinese specialists, but there are many of you who are not.

"Now. In China, people are very sensitive about not losing face. Not losing face means to keep others from losing respect for oneself or to avoid embarrassment. Their social status as perceived by others is nearly as crucial to them as money is to us. If we embarrass any of them, they will feel as if we robbed them."

Darren saw a hand go up, and he pointed at the woman and said, "Yes, please go ahead."

"What kinds of comments would make them feel as if they'd lost face?"

Darren nodded. "Good question. The Chinese will feel slighted if you make them feel as if whatever they just said is either false or ridiculous. An easy remedy for this is to acknowledge at least some grain of truth in their statements. Any other questions before I continue?"

A large military man raised his hand and asked, "Why are they so concerned with saving face? Respectfully, aren't we here to come to some kind of reconciliation over the South China Sea fiasco? That seems more important than feelings."

"I understand your perspective," Darren said politely, "but China's history is such that they will always value saving face, regardless of the circumstances. Historically, China has been exploited by foreign nations who had colonized the country for economic reasons. Because of this, they are sensitive to appearing as submissive or as being dominated by Westerners. For the majority of the last two hundred years, the West was dominant over China, both economically and politically. Now, the two powers are far more balanced, and the Chinese are determined not to fall back into their inferior status of yesteryear. They expect respect from us.

"In Chinese culture, the concept of face signifies the amount of dignity or prestige associated with an individual. The twentieth-century Chinese writer Lu Xun defined 'face' as 'the guiding principle of the Chinese mind.' In his writings, he recognizes the difficulty foreigners have in truly embracing this idea. He gave an illustrative historical example of the concept that I'd like to share. During the Qing Dynasty, which endured from 1644 to 1912, foreigners would approach the foreign ministry of imperial China to submit requests. If they were declined, then they would threaten the Chinese officials, who then acquiesced out of fear. Still, the Chinese officials would release the foreigners through a side door, rather than through the main door. This symbolized that the foreigners had no face in the eyes of the Chinese. You see, it's all about respect. The Chinese remember slights against them. Any questions or comments?"

A well-dressed woman in business attire towards the back of the room—who was well-known as a legal expert on the laws of the seas—raised her hand and asked, "I know that Confucianism has had a lasting influence on Chinese culture. Is there anything we need to know with respect to that ideology?"

"Yes," Darren said confidently. "I intended to get to that a bit later, but I'll mention it now. Many of China's contemporary social values stem from ancient Confucian teachings, which valorized the submission of the individual to the family unit and even larger collectives. Also, Confucius and his pupils preached benevolence and filial piety. Relationships are sanctified in Confucianism, especially those between the emperor and his subject, father and son, husband and wife, and friends. In general, Confucianism glorifies society as a whole far more than the American tradition of individualism. We need to appreciate this difference as we proceed into negotiations."

A sea of faces nodded at him, and Darren smiled. "Good. I want to now shift gears and talk about some Chinese geopolitical history. I'm going to discuss a territorial dispute that China had with Japan over the Senkaku Islands, to give you an idea of how China regards oceanic territorial disputes in general. Senkaku Islands are a group of uninhabited islands in the East China Sea. They are located northeast of Taiwan, east of China, west of Okinawa Island. China claims the discovery and ownership of the islands dating back to the fourteenth century. Meanwhile, Japan controlled the islands from 1895 until the country's surrender at the end of World War II, with a brief period of U.S. intervention that doesn't concern us now. The People's Republic of China began questioning the sovereignty of these islands in 1970, when they discovered that they may have harbored oil reserves. I see a hand. Yes, you in the back. What's your question?"

"I remember learning about this dispute in graduate school. Didn't Taiwan also claim the islands for itself?"

"Yes, very good. China claims historical right to Taiwan. Not only does this territory house oil reserves, but it is also close to critical shipping lanes and bountiful fishing grounds, so everyone wanted a piece of it. China argued that evidence indicated that the territory was China's rightful possession, and that Japan had merely seized it for themselves many years ago. China demanded that the territory be returned to them just as the rest of Imperial Japan's conquests were returned at the end of World War II.

"Now, the United States became involved through the Treaty of Mutual Cooperation and Security between the United States and Japan, which stipulated that the United States had to help Japan in any military defense of these islands. The treaty is strictly between the United States and Japan. I see a hand. Yes?"

A gentleman with a shaved head asked, "I'm confused. Didn't Japan buy some of these islands?"

"Yes," Darren replied. "I'm trying to only give you the most important details. In 2020, the Japanese government indeed purchased the islands from the Kurihara family, after which angry protests exploded in China. Tensions rose, and it has been said that the conflict over the islands was the greatest risk for war between

China and Japan since the time of World War II. I don't need to spell out the parallels between that situation and our own for you all."

There was a tense period of silence. After a few beats, Darren continued. "I want to tell you all about one more piece of history, this one very recent. There have been reports that China might try to coercively bring Taiwan back under its rule within the next decade. In response to this hypothetical, our own Congress has allocated billions of dollars to the Pacific Deterrence Initiative. According to some experts, it's a little too late to rebuild U.S. preponderance and restore deterrence. Still, this initiative will increase U.S. capacity to win a war by convincing China that it would choose to fight in the face of Chinese provocations. Yes, you, in the front?"

A woman with long, brown hair said, "I heard that our marine corps is ratcheting up its presence in Asia, too. Is that true?"

"It is. They recently finished the construction of a new base in Guam, the first since the 1950s. The navy, marine corps, and air force have more extensive plans, too, but I won't trouble you with the details. Their goal is to make it easier for American forces to engage in 'island-hopping' operations in Asia, so that they can neutralize Chinese targets faster than ever before."

"Do we have a mutual defense treaty for Taiwan?" someone in the front asked.

"No, but we may have an obligation to defend. It is the president's decision."

"Why is America involved in that region, in the first place?" a man sitting on the right-hand side of the room asked without raising his hand.

"The United States has allies in the region—such as Japan, South Korea, the Philippines, and Australia—and several mutual defense obligations," Darren answered. "We have always supported democracies. Currently, both China and the United States are in a dangerous dance, in which one side increases its military footprint and the other follows suit. I see a hand. Yes, sir?"

"If we did go to war with China over Taiwan, do you think we could win?"

"Let me answer this," Bill said forwardly. "I'll be honest. I'm not sure. China has greatly expanded their naval, air, and missile forces over the past twenty-five years. They are now deploying advanced weaponry and technology. Furthermore, fighting a defensive campaign close to home bases gives them a great advantage. But it's important to remember that they would be willing to bear a far higher cost in order to annex Taiwan as a breakaway province than we would be willing to bear in defending it. They see pulling Taiwan into their reign as a way to defend China's sovereignty and territorial integrity. Even in the best-case scenario, a war with China would have the potential to exact a heavy toll on U.S. ships and aircrafts projecting power towards China. We can no longer expect a swift, cheap victory in a war with China in the Western Pacific. In the worst-case scenario, our countries could attack each other with nuclear weapons, resulting in the destruction of cities and the loss of millions of innocent lives in both countries.

"China is a formidable force, my friends. Remember that when we begin your negotiations today. Best of luck, and Godspeed."

While the Americans had their morning meeting, their Chinese counterparts met in a different room.

"My friends," Yao began, speaking at a podium to his dozens of diplomats, "thank you for joining me on this vital occasion. As you know, we will be speaking with America's diplomats in short order. Before I let my aide, Mr. Wang Fang, speak, I want to remind you all that our territory in the South China Sea must remain in our possession. Some of you may not know that about one-third of the world's merchandise goes through the sea's channels. Therefore, not only as our patriotic duty, but also for basic economic reasons, we must not settle for anything less than domination of the region. Now, I welcome Wang Fang to the stage."

A tall and handsome man took Yao's place at the podium. He ran his fingers through slicked-back hair, adjusted his expensive suit jacket, and spoke into the microphone. "Thank you, Foreign Minister. And thank you all for your service. I want to put today's upcoming negotiations in historical context.

"The earliest event I want to remind you of is the Shanghai International Settlement. This began in 1843 with the Treaty of Nanking that was signed after the British imperialists defeated the Qing army in the First Opium War. The treaty mandated that Shanghai would serve as a treaty port open to foreign businessmen. I emphasize that the treaty forced the Qing Dynasty to make territorial and economic concessions to the British. It also forced our country to let British merchants sell opium to our citizens, which caused many deaths and ruined families. To add insult to injury, they even made us pay for the opium that we destroyed in the war we fought to protect our citizens.

"The Americans followed Great Britain's lead and established their own enclaves in China, north of those of the British. The Americans signed treaties with China that gave Americans special privileges within China.

"In Shanghai, Great Britain and the United States collaborated to form the Shanghai International Settlement. In 1863, the previously distinct enclaves of the two powers in Shanghai merged, such that both powers' citizens would benefit from being able to live in Shanghai while being held only answerable to their native country's legal code.

"This ability to colonize our country and remain outside the jurisdiction of our own legal code is one way by which the Americans have demonstrated disrespect towards us. Before I move on, are there any questions?"

Wang pointed to a woman with her hand up near the front of the room.

"Didn't the United States fight on our side during World War II?"

"Yes," Wang replied, "which makes their imperialism even more tragic. To your point, there was the famous First American Volunteer Group of the Republic of China Air Force in the early 1940s, also called the Flying Tigers. These were pilots from the American army air corps, navy, and marine corps. The American president at the time, Franklin Roosevelt, authorized these forces to fight for China before Japan attacked Pearl Harbor. You may have seen images of their aircrafts, painted with shark jaws and the Republic of China's national flag but flown by Americans. I see another hand. Yes?"

A man asked, "Did they make a significant impact in the war?"

"Good question. Admittedly, they were rather underfunded. They had only a handful of doctors on staff, and the pilots had only forty-five maintenance staff personally on hand, rather than the usual hundred or more. Despite their paucity of resources, though, they brought down nearly three hundred of our enemy's aircrafts. Any other questions? If not, I want to move on.

"As you know, China underwent a civil war from 1927 to 1949, as the government of the Republic of China fought with our Communist Party of China for control of our nation. After World War II, the United States supported the nationalist government, led by Chiang Kai-shek, against our great leader, Mao Zedong. They did so in order to prevent the rise of communism in our nation."

Wang saw a woman's hand go up, and he pointed at her silently.

"The United States backed the nationalists, right?"

"Indeed. However, their financial and military backing proved inadequate, and in 1949, Mao Zedong founded the People's Republic of China. Chiang and his people fled to Taiwan, planning to recapture mainland China at a later date.

"Our great leader struggled to find agreement with the United States over important issues. In 1949, their administration, under Harry Truman, published the 'China White Paper' that explained that only Chinese people could determine China's political fate. This understandably angered the exiled nationalist government and army in Taiwan, who had previously enjoyed help from the Western power. I see a hand. What is your question?"

"Didn't we and the U.S. fight on separate sides in the Korean War?" a man with a long beard asked. "I ask because Taiwan became entangled in this, right?"

"That's right," Wang said. "The United States, still under Truman, worked to ensure that the Korean War did not spill over into Taiwan. This initiated a U.S. policy of protecting Chiang Kai-shek's government in Taiwan.

"I remind you all of these historic events so that you remember that the United States will always be a self-interested nation. If they intervene in our affairs, it is because they either want our resources or because they regard our ideas as invalid. They have intruded enough in our internal quarrels. Do not let them get away with it again."

THIRTEEN
★★★
CHAPTER

T he American diplomats, with Admiral Smith aggressively leading, walked purposefully down the lodge's hallway on the second floor. They all wore white shirts, black suits, and plain red or blue ties. As they headed towards the conference room, they walked by a lineup of Chinese staff members, who greeted them. Bill noticed several armed security guards, positioned at regular intervals.

Josh yawned as they approached the massive wooden double doors of the conference room. "The coffee in the room is weak."

"Yes," Bill said. "It's hard to reverse your body clock. My body tells me that I should be sleeping now."

A sign on the door had a couple of Chinese characters on it, as well as its English translation. "Grand Room," Thomas read aloud. "Seems fitting."

From the other side of the hall, the Chinese diplomats appeared. The ones at the front of the pack waved to the Americans, who responded in kind.

"Good morning, all," Yao said. Then he helped open the doors and gestured for everyone to enter the Grand Room.

At the front of the room, Bill saw a large banner that said, "WELCOME SECRETARY OF STATE WILLIAM BRYERS AND DIPLOMATS." The rest of the room was occupied by several large, circular tables with about fifteen seats each. On each table lay a map of the South China Sea. Even with a quick glance, Bill noticed that most of the sea was marked as belonging to Chinese territory—the red coloring gave it away.

A dozen or so small windows on the far side of the room gave Bill a view of the cold morning outside, which offered a beautiful visual of the Great Wall.

China has been around for over four thousand years, Bill thought. *The wall is a testament to their ability to play the long game.*

He took the view in for a peaceful moment before taking a seat. The rest of the diplomats followed suit until they formed a circle.

Anticipating yet another moment of awkward silence, Bill asked Yao, "We'll all be facing each other?"

Yao nodded soberly. "We find it most conducive to discussions. It engenders a conciliatory mood."

Bill clasped his hands together under the table. "Minister, I respectfully disagree. We need a long table so that each diplomat may sit directly across from his or her counterpart."

Yao shook his head. "Perhaps next time, Secretary."

Bill sighed but yielded the point. *In the peace negotiations during the Vietnam War, an argument over the shape of the negotiating table took nine months to settle. We don't have that kind of time.*

Then he pulled a map from his jacket's internal pocket and laid it out on the table. "This is a map of the South China Sea and its international waters, which our ship was clearly in."

Yao frowned. "That is not correct."

Before Bill could continue, the doors to the Grand Room opened. Several staff members entered, holding trays filled with cups and a single teapot. As the staff served the diplomats tea and cookies, Bill smiled at Yao.

"Oh, thank God," Thomas said.

"Guo-tea is a great Chinese tradition," Yao said. "Tea was discovered by Chinese Emperor Shennong in 2738 BC of your calendar. A leaf from a nearby shrub fell into boiling water, and the water tasted good. Tea is a big part of our culture."

The group nodded and sipped their tea. Once the staff exited the Grand Room, Yao said, "Now, we may begin in earnest. Mr. Secretary, since you are our guests, please present first."

Bill thought that Yao sounded more relaxed than he had only a minute ago. *I guess some elements of human nature are universal,* he thought. *A hot drink relaxes everyone, American, Chinese, and otherwise.* Then Bill turned to Admiral Smith. "Go ahead."

Smith rose to his feet and approached the front of the room, where the U.S. delegation had hung up a map. He took a laser pointer out from his pocket and directed a light beam on a point on the map that was sprawled across the table. "You can see here—"

"Those are Chinese waters!" Commander Wong interrupted angrily.

Smith's face reddened. "Do not interrupt me again, commander."

Bill's heart began to beat more quickly. "Admiral Smith," he said calmly, "please, continue."

"As I was saying," Smith growled. "Here is where good Americans were killed by Chinese forces in international waters."

Commander Wong slammed his fists down on the table. "What is this? How dare you disrespect us! This whole debacle began with *your* mistakes, not ours! You shot missiles at our jets first!"

Bill looked to Yao, who put a hand on Wong's shoulder. "Commander, please. Now is not the time for outrage."

"Enough about where to cast the blame," Bill said. "Admiral Smith, please return to your seat." Bill pointed to a spot on the map and said, "Minister, do you concede that our ships had the right to be here in these international waters?"

Yao shook his head. "No. U.S. ships don't have that right, and any attack on them is justified after we were attacked in our waters. I'm sorry, Secretary, but you must come to recognize China as a superpower in her own right. We won't be pushed around by the United States anymore, like when you forced a one-sided treaty on us after we lost the Opium Wars in the 1800s. You can't do whatever you want. What if the Chinese Navy was two hundred miles from San Francisco? We are equal to America. As such, we will not budge on any territorial dispute regarding the South China Sea."

Bill banged his hands on the table. "We will not allow these international waters to be China's." He pointed to the disputed Chinese waters on the map as he spoke.

"Answer my question," Yao demanded. "What if the Chinese Navy does practice drills two hundred miles from San Francisco or New York?"

"No," Bill said, his voice hard and steady.

"I see. In other words, America may roam wherever she pleases, but this privilege will never be granted to any other superpower. And a superpower we are, Secretary Bryers."

"Our navy is not there to threaten China," Admiral Smith interjected, "but to protect the freedom of navigation of ships and cargo, in addition to protecting our allies in the region."

"How convenient a framework," Commander Wong replied venomously. "Your reasons are righteous, ours nefarious. I guess you are protecting them from us. But we are not threatening anyone. China has no recent history of foreign wars, yet the United States has a long history of invading countries—just recently, Vietnam, Iraq, and Afghanistan."

"Let's talk about rights," Bill intervened. "While the accident in the South China Sea was regretful, we had every right to pass through—"

"*Every right?*" Yao said, in shock. "That's our territory!"

"Your air force should not be flying overhead or near our navy," Bill responded. "This type of accident was bound to happen, as these war games are going on nearly daily. Come on, Minister. At least acknowledge that we were in international waters!"

Yao crossed his arms defensively. "I will do no such thing!"

Wong pounded a fist into his open palm in anger. He rose to his feet, and Bill followed suit. The pair of leaders stared into each other's eyes, each waiting for the other to blink. Yao turned his gaze towards the doors and walked briskly in their direction.

"I'll get him," Chen said, and caught up to Yao before he could leave the room. They exchanged fierce whispers, while the rest of the diplomats sat uncomfortably in their seats.

Sara, who was sitting next to Bill, nudged him and whispered, "This isn't going anywhere."

Bill noticed that all of the Americans were looking at him. "Don't worry. Negotiations can start like this sometimes."

"Do they ever end like this?" Josh asked.

Bill did not answer.

"Ladies and gentlemen," Yao announced, still standing by the door with Chen, "I think we should take a break. Why doesn't everyone go to the lobby? They'll have breakfast shortly."

"Minister," Bill said, "I'm not sure that's necessary. Why don't you come sit down?"

Yao held up a hand. "I insist. We'll return to the Grand Room in two hours."

As Bill entered the lobby, he felt a tap on his shoulder. "Sir?"

Bill turned to see the lodge concierge. He looked nervous. "A woman called for you. She said to call her back immediately. Do you need the number?"

"No, I know who it is. But thank you. Do you have a phone I could use?"

The concierge nodded. "Yes, of course. Please, come to the front desk."

Bill picked up the landline that the concierge offered him and dialed his daughter's phone number. "H-hello?" a female voice said shakily.

"Hey, it's me," Bill said quickly to his daughter. "What's wrong?"

"It's Jack," the woman said. Bill could hear her tears through the line. "He's dead. It's confirmed. A friend of his saw his dead body floating in the water."

"What?"

She sobbed. "I don't know what to do—"

"Oh my god," Bill breathed.

Sara approached Bill, who looked at her through tear-blurred vision. "Honey, I have to go. Who is with you?"

"Tommy, Mom, and the whole family."

"I'm sorry. I love you, and I'm not going to let China get away with this. Do you hear me? Everything will be fine. I need you to breathe and take every minute at a time. Okay? I love you. Goodbye."

"Bill," Sara said, as she put a delicate hand on his arm. "Is everything alright?"

"My son-in-law is dead," Bill said flatly. He suddenly felt like he was in a dream. "Jack. He was on the ship that the Chinese sunk." Sara's eyes widened as she saw anger distort her boss's face. "They killed him, Sara."

"Okay, Bill. Okay. But we need to keep levelheaded now."

Bill sharply pulled Sara's hand off his arm. "Do we? Or maybe Jack would want us to blow them to kingdom come!"

"You know that we need to try to deescalate this. Tensions are already high. It's the right thing to do."

"I guess I lost my temper yesterday with the loss of my son-in-law," Bill began, as tears slid down his cheeks. "I really should work to resolve this crisis. Look, Sara, go eat. I need to be alone now. I'll see you when our session reconvenes."

FOURTEEN

★ ★ ★

CHAPTER

Qingdao, China

Russian Vice President Dmitry Petrov gazed out at the city of Qingdao from the large office window. He was well aware that the city was part of a German-leased territory from 1898 until the outbreak of World War I in 1914.

He stood in a Qingdao tower, which was owned by an international construction company, whose major owner, in turn, was the Chinese government. From the top floor of the building, he could see the curved coastline of the Chinese city and the beautiful greenery that hugged the shore. In stark contrast with the natural scenery was historic eighteenth- and nineteenth-century German architecture that stood further inland. To Dmitry's far right, he saw the famous Port of Qingdao against the Yellow Sea. He was impressed with its sheer size: the rows of tankers, ships, and carriers seemingly went on forever.

Qingdao Port's container terminal is the most advanced terminal on the planet, Dmitry thought. *And it is Asia's first totally automated terminal facility.*

The ships' red-and-white colors reminded Dmitry who he was dealing with.

Dmitry caught his own reflection in the glass pane he'd been looking through. He looked tired, with noticeable bags under his small, dark eyes. Tall, thin, and pale, he ran a hand through his thinning, slicked-back hair in the hopes that he'd appear more alert.

"Have you been to Qingdao before?" a voice said in Russian but with a Chinese accent from behind Dmitry.

The Russian turned around to see a short man in his forties dressed in what was clearly a naval uniform. "Yes," Dmitry replied. "Although I am impressed every time. It reminds me of the American port town San Diego. I spent years spying on their naval base in San Diego. They are so unprotected." He put his hand out. "I am deputy Dmitry Petrov, here to represent Russia's president."

"I am Chinese naval officer Kong Luoyang. I understand your leader wished to communicate with us regarding our latest conflict with the United States."

Dmitry gestured towards the view of Qingdao, as if Kong had not spoken. "Qingdao was colonized by Germany around the turn of the twentieth century, correct?"

Kong nodded. "That is right. To this day, many German cultural artifacts remain in our city. Perhaps you will witness some of them tonight. The Germans built their own streets, sewers, electrical systems, and missionary schools during their time here. I don't know if you enjoy alcohol, but our world-famous Tsingtao Brewery was originally founded by the Germans in 1903."

"They chose this city for a reason," Dmitry replied. "Your port was strategically significant a century ago, and it remains so during this tense episode. If memory serves me well, the German naval forces made great use of your port."

"Mr. Petrov, if I may inquire, why do you broach our history?"

Dmitry smiled mirthlessly. "You strike me as a no-nonsense man. I respect that. We wish to help you against the Americans. Before you ask, our motivations are simple. Russia and China are friends. We are allies in despising the idea of the United States dictating to us how we should run our sovereign countries."

Kong's expression did not change. "I appreciate your candor. How do you propose to aid us?"

"Let us sell you weaponry. We can deliver them directly to your naval base here. This is the headquarters of the People's Liberation Army Navy's North Sea Fleet. You will need advanced naval weaponry to fight the Americans."

Kong took a pensive breath before responding. "You are correct that Qingdao has been a very important location to world powers for a long time. The Japanese empire occupied it for a time, in addition to the Germans. Following World War I, our ancestors did not take kindly to the Paris Peace Conference's decision not to remove foreign occupation of Qingdao. The city has been under Chinese control since Mao Zedong took it in 1949, and we intend for it to remain our own. Know that, Mr. Petrov."

Dmitry placed his hands out in a placating gesture. "Without a doubt, good sir. We only offer our support against the Americans. I know they did wrong by you—the South China Sea is not their territory to meddle in. We only offer our allegiance." Dmitry wagged a finger. "No deception. No trickery. We anticipate that friendship with China is a long-term investment." Dmitry placed his hand out for Kong to shake. "What do you say?"

Kong took a step closer to the Russian and shook his hand. "Nothing is official until tonight, you understand. Further deliberations are required, many of which will occur at our dinner. But yes, I do accept your offer."

Dmitry smiled again. "Excellent. May you continue to reign in the South China Sea and in the Pacific."

They toasted each other with Qingdao beer.

Yokosuka, Japan

Admiral Blackstone sat in the gray room, idly rotating his coffee cup in his hand. He struggled to put on a friendly face as the Japanese naval officer took a seat on the other side of the table.

"This coffee is a bit bitter for my taste," the admiral grunted.

The Japanese man opened his mouth a few times before responding, "Shall I get you another?"

Blackstone shook his head. "No worries, Officer Watanabe. I needed the mental break from our talks as much as the caffeine. But we're making progress. Let's get back into it."

Watanabe took a delicate sip of his tea before returning his attention to the American. "Yes. As I said, we have taken an interest in the rising tension in the South China Sea. As we speak, your navy and China's are facing each other. We do not want China to retain control of the islands in the South China Sea. Moreover, via landfill, they are manufacturing new islands in order to claim additional sea territory. We are concerned with China's growing influence. We were once imperialistic, and we do not want to ever be under the thumb of Chinese communists. Furthermore, your nation and ours are bound together by a mutual defense treaty. I want the United States to end the threat now, before my people are forced to involve ourselves militarily."

Blackstone stroked his chin. "The Treaty of Mutual Cooperation and Security between the United States and Japan has lasted for over sixty years in its current incarnation. I understand your perspective. If we engage in battle with China in the South China Sea, would you join us?"

"It depends," Watanabe responded. "But I can promise you that we would at least support you with resources. Perhaps because you live on the other side of the world, you have not yet come to appreciate just how powerful China is becoming. I insist that you fight sooner rather than later. Yes, halting China's ascension would benefit Japan and the United States. But my point is that if you wait even five years to fight them, you may lose. You are very likely to win a war with them now. In five years, I do not know if you would succeed."

After a pause, Blackstone said, "If I'm remembering correctly, our treaty says that if there is an attack on either of our territories around Japan proper, both of our countries should act. But … I remember reading that your own constitution forbids the use of force when resolving international disputes."

Watanabe smiled. "You are more learned than you appear, Admiral, and I mean that sincerely. Your General MacArthur, who ruled Japan during the United States occupation after World War II, insisted on a new constitution that mandates nonaggression. That is why we rely on the U.S. to protect us from aggressors. There was an addendum to our nations' treaty with precisely this constraint in mind. Rest assured that if there is an attack on any of the islands in our aegis, we are bound to help each other. And before you ask: even if

China attacks you outside of our orbit, we can help you economically, and possibly through military action."

"That is quite gracious of you. We also have mutual defense treaties with South Korea. Leveraging these treaties gives me pause, Watanabe. World War I was global in scope precisely *because* the countries who fought were bound to each other in a complex web of alliances. I worry that the same thing would happen if we duke it out with China. We cannot give up on diplomacy."

"I agree," Watanabe said. "And we want you to succeed. But know that Japan is behind you in the event that you fight. I imagine Taiwan is, too."

Blackstone took a sip of his coffee and ignored the bitter taste in his mouth. "If diplomacy fails, we may have your support. We may even have South Korea's and Taiwan's. But I suspect that China would not be alone on the other side. North Korea is just waiting to invade South Korea. Tunnels from North Korea have been discovered all over the border. They were capable of moving twenty thousand troops across it in an hour. I hope that they have discovered all of them. I know the American in charge of the negotiations with the Chinese. He's a good man. But honor won't cut it, this time. I hope he's talented enough to pull off a peace deal, or this is going to get real ugly, real quick."

South China Sea

Admiral Miller stood in the cabin of the USS *Zumwalt*, one of the largest and most advanced warships of the U.S. Navy. He paced back and forth with his hands behind his back, hoping that he could hide his nerves by remaining in motion.

"Miller," a deep yet feminine voice said from across the room.

The admiral turned to find Admiral Dennett standing across the hall, looking both mean and stoic at the same time. "Yes, Admiral Dennett?"

"The Chinese have moved closer towards us."

After an awkward pause, Miller asked, "Do you want my opinion?"

"Obviously."

"Let's keep a safe distance to avoid battle. We need to wait on orders."

Dennett's eyes swept over Miller's person like a predator discovering its prey. "We have the USS *Zumwalt* here, ready to fire at a moment's notice. She possesses state-of-the-art electric propulsion systems, stealth design, and impressive weaponry. She's only a few years old. We should make use of her."

Miller put his hands in his pockets and looked down at his shoes. "And USS *John S. McCain* has recently joined the fray. She has a pretty intense history, you know. She was deployed to the Persian Gulf in 2003 and launched over three dozen Tomahawk missiles during the Iraq invasion."

"I'm a fan of USS *Curtis Wilbur*," Dennett said. "She has history in these waters. As recently as 2016, she participated in a series of operations ensuring freedom of navigation in the South China Sea."

"The size and strength of our fleet should intimidate the Chinese. But let's be careful not to start a war."

"You're faint of heart, Miller," Dennett said with a disapproving tone. "But maybe you have a point. Once the bloodshed starts, it won't stop for a long, long time."

Miller swallowed and looked back up at Dennett, who was grinning hungrily. "I pray it doesn't come to that."

South China Sea

"They call them 'Little Blue Men,'" Commander Yi said.

Commander Dong swallowed the last piece of his biscuit before responding. "Westerners have always been paranoid about our maritime militia."

"I read that they think our 'Little Blue Men' are hundreds of boats directly controlled by Beijing that our government uses to reinforce our territorial claims in the South China Sea. But the Westerners are lashing out in full paranoia."

Dong looked around the small dining area of their ship. "No matter. They are the invaders. Regardless of the conspiracies that they spew, we will no longer allow them to imperialize our waters."

"We have automatic weapons on some of our ships, as well as reinforced hulls. At close range, they don't stand a chance."

Dong laughed confidently. "We have the world's largest navy. And we have an armed fishing force! The Americans are alien to our ways of controlling these waters. You know America's greatest weakness?"

Yi frowned. "Its opulence?"

Dong shook his head. "Its *arrogance*. The Americans cannot fathom alternative worldviews, alternative cultures, nor alternative solutions. Their parochialism will be their downfall. It's time we shook the scales from their eyes. By force."

"What are you saying, commander?"

"That it is time to flex our might for the Americans to see. No more sitting passively. We have a paramilitary force of ships and armed fishing vessels all over the South China Sea."

Yi leaned in towards Dong. "No fighting. Not yet."

Dong smiled wolfishly. "We don't have to aggress against the Americans to scare them. But scare them we will."

Yi took a long time before he responded. "Okay. Let's do it."

"I hope we receive orders to fight. We can finally show the Americans that we can defend ourselves."

FIFTEEN
★★★
CHAPTER

B ill wiped the tears from his eyes as he held his secured satellite phone against his ear, trying desperately to push away painful thoughts about his family.

I have a job to do, he thought. *These are matters of global importance. My personal life has to take a back seat. I don't have a choice.*

"Gary Rhodes," a young, masculine voice said on the other end. "Who's calling?"

"Hello. This is Secretary of State Bill Bryers. I'd like to speak with the president, please. He's expecting my call."

"Please stay on the line."

"Thank you."

Bill looked out of the window of his lodge room as he waited. He noticed that thick clouds were forming, the kind that often preceded heavy snowfall.

"Secretary Bryers. How are you?"

"Mr. President, thank you for taking my call. I—"

"Before you begin," the president said authoritatively, "I'm going to connect our entire National Security Council."

Bill blinked. He hadn't expected such a large audience, although he had enough experience to handle them. "Yes, of course."

After a few seconds and a *beep*, a slow, feminine voice said, "Hello, Secretary Bryers. This is Chairman of the Joint Chiefs of Staff, Kara Shipley."

"Yes. I hope you're well this … late at night."

"You're on speaker," Kara said. "The rest of the National Security Council can hear you. Have you met with the Chinese yet?"

Bill took a breath and gathered his thoughts. "Yes. It did not go well. Frankly, we barely got off the ground. They refused to concede that our forces are in international waters. They claim that most of the South China Sea is their rightful territory."

"Did they seem open to compromise?" Kara asked.

Bill shook his head. "Honestly, we couldn't even get into possible solutions. One of their commanders claimed that we disrespected them merely by stating the fact that they killed some Americans."

"Secretary," the president said, "did you get a sense of their attitude? Did they seem confident in their position, or were they threatened by us?"

Bill recalled Yao's words from their meeting. "Truly, I wish I had better news. But it doesn't seem like we're dealing with a paper tiger, so far as I can tell. They were quite adamant about their status as a global superpower. I insisted that the United States would not allow China to run roughshod over the disputed waters, but they grandstanded at that. Claimed the moral high ground."

"Their arrogance will be their undoing," Kara said. "What's your next move, Secretary?"

"We're going to meet again very soon. I'm hoping to earn some concessions from the Chinese. Maybe they'll be calmer."

"Don't give them an inch," the president seethed. "I can't believe they think they have the right to rule over international waters. What did they say, in particular?"

"For one thing," Bill responded, "they invoked our invasions of Vietnam, Iraq, and Afghanistan, claiming that we are aggressors in foreign wars, while they've never been aggressors. They also likened the situation at the South China Sea to one in which the Chinese Navy is two hundred miles from San Francisco."

"They certainly sound confident," Kara muttered. "Unbearable and sanctimonious, as well. Secretary, *do not* back down. Our navy is heading into the South China Sea as we speak. They will be ready to respond militarily if they are fired upon. They might talk a good game, but they don't hold a candle to our might."

Bill swallowed. Doubt was creeping into his mind, and he couldn't shake it. "Are you sure that's necessary?" he asked.

"Yes, Secretary," Kara said with a pinch of condescension. "By all means, continue to negotiate with the Chinese. I hope you succeed.

But we cannot naively hope that words will be enough. Surely you understand."

Bill thought about his daughter and how much pain she was in. *Will the violence ever end?*

"Yes, I understand."

"Thank you for your time, Secretary," the president said. "Best of luck in the next round of negotiations. Godspeed."

"Thank you, Mr. President."

Yao took a sip of his tea, set it down, and lay on his bed, careful not to wrinkle his professional clothes. He knew what he had to do, but he needed a moment in relaxed silence. He had forgotten how intense diplomatic negotiations could be. At his age, it drained him not only mentally but physically as well.

After a few minutes, he willed himself to pick up the phone and make the call.

"Hello?"

"This is Foreign Minister Yao Sheng. I hope I haven't interrupted anything."

"Not at all."

"The first round of negotiations with the Americans did not go well at all. Commander Wong grew very angry, very quickly. I do not blame him. The American delegates were extremely entitled in their mindset."

"What happened?"

"The Americans insisted that we concede that our part of the South China Sea is international waters. Commander Wong stormed out of the room, and the American leader, Secretary of State Bill Bryers, did the same."

"Are you optimistic about the negotiations moving forward?"

Yao sighed. "I'm not sure. It was so tense … and the Americans seem religiously bound to their double standard. The tone was very confrontational. They think that *they* get to be the world's police, but if any other superpower engages in similar activity, then those other nations are necessarily in the wrong. I don't think I can persuade them out of this mindset in such short order."

"You need to swim with the tide, Yao. Not against it."

"What do you mean?"

"You have identified the nature of the enemy. Don't bother resisting it. You yourself admitted that such a task is impossible. Think of a way to use it to your advantage."

Yao thought hard about what his interlocutor was saying. "I am happy to feed the Americans' ego, but I'm not sure the other diplomats would be happy with that. As I said, we have some hotheads on our side."

"Yao, you've been a hero of China for decades. Everyone who knows you respects what you've done. It's time for one last bout of leadership. I have faith in you."

Yao smiled faintly and took another sip of his tea. "Thank you for the kind words. Our second round of negotiations is approaching. I should go."

"One last thing, Yao. We are not going to depend solely on diplomacy to defeat the Americans. Know that if they come into our sovereign part of the South China Sea, we will attack."

"Military action is unnecessary," Yao said quickly. "Bloodshed is not an option."

"Respectfully, that is not your decision to make. It *is* an option. And for perhaps the first time in human history, with our new weapons technology we have the power to defeat the American empire in battle, once and for all."

Yao did not know what to say. "I have to go now. Thank you for speaking with me."

Faces were taut and tensions were high as the American and Chinese diplomats filled into the Grand Room once more. Everyone took the exact same seat as they had the last time.

The silence was as awkward as it was heated. After a few heavy seconds, Yao said, "I hope your break gave you the space you needed."

"Same to you," Bill replied politely.

Yao nodded. "I'd like to open with an admission. The United States is a world superpower. There is no doubt about it. You have done a lot of good across the world. I recognize that you have enjoyed a position of singular superpower over the last several decades, especially since the end of the Cold War."

"Thank you for the kind words, Minister," Bill said. "At the risk of sounding rude, why are you confirming what everyone already knows?"

"Because times are changing, Secretary. The norms under a world order of Western domination do not apply anymore. There are other considerations that you will have to take into account."

"Like what?" Bill asked with just a slight edge.

"That you are no longer the only superpower in the field. That you cannot disregard our wishes in territorial disputes any longer."

"I won't stand for this," Admiral Smith said quietly, but with authority. "You speak as if our nations are the same. You are run by a communist party. We are a proud democracy. You mentioned the Cold War. Would you say that the Soviet Union and the United States were simply two superpowers engaged in a global battle for supremacy? Or can you admit that one party was objectively evil and the other good?"

Bill turned his head to the admiral with a look of disapproval.

"The admiral has a point," Yao responded calmly. "But to answer your question, I regard the fall of the Soviet Union as a tragedy. I'm not sure the rise of America is any less of one."

Admiral Smith rose from his feet. "Enough disrespect! You cloak your disdain for us in passive-aggressive compliments. I ain't buying it! Will you compensate us for the Americans that you killed, or not?"

"Admiral," Bill thundered. "Take a seat. Minister, have you decided to make some kind of offer?"

All eyes were on Yao. After a pause, he said quietly, "You don't want to push us."

"What?" Bill snapped. "What did you say?"

"As I said, times have changed. If you impose yourselves on us in the South China Sea, you will lose. I don't want it to come to that. So please, Secretary. Back down. Have your forces leave the South China Sea while there is still peace."

Bill thought of his dead son-in-law. *Peace has already come and gone.*

"We can't allow the families of those poor, innocent Americans to receive no justice," Bill said indignantly. "Will you offer recompense to the families of the men and women who died in the South China Sea?" He pointed to the map and added, "Will your navy cease harassing our navy here in the international waters?"

Yao shook his head, his expression flat. "If we agree to offer packages to the families of the fallen Americans, we would be admitting that we were in the wrong. I'm truly sorry, but that is not an option."

Commander Wong suddenly burst out laughing.

Admiral Smith stood up again. "How dare you!" he yelled at Wong. "You disrespectful *coward!*"

A sense of defeat overcame Bill. Just as he opened his mouth to speak, another Chinese diplomat yelled back at Smith, "You imperialist warmonger!"

A young American diplomat called back, "Communist!"

More and more voices erupted in a cacophony of accusations, hostility, and name-calling.

Bill's heart sank as he faced the painful realization that neither side would budge. He made eye contact with Yao, whose expression was too stony for Bill to get a read on.

The secretary of state stood and clapped his hands together with the kind of authoritative thunder that only came with experience. Everyone immediately stopped yelling and turned to him.

"That's enough. I can see that you have placed your own pride before finding a solution."

"I could say the same about you, Secretary," Yao responded.

"I apologize to all the diplomats here. This has been an utter waste of time. We'll leave this lodge in the morning and return to our country. When you want to seriously negotiate, you can come to Washington."

There were some audible gasps, but Bill kept his eyes on Yao. "We won't forget your insults, Foreign Minister."

Yao gestured towards the door. "You've made your thoughts clear. Please, if you want an end to our summit, go ahead. Leave."

Bill nodded. "That's it, then. Come on, everyone. Our negotiations have ended. We'll take a flight to Washington tomorrow morning."

SIXTEEN
★★★
CHAPTER

ao walked out of the back of the hotel and into a beautiful garden. There, he stepped onto a Chinese pagoda bridge that took him towards a traditional teahouse. He took a seat in the house's opening room, and he saw that the room was connected to a few other rooms via open doorways. Yao knew that the entire layout was meant for relaxation and contemplation, which were just what he needed right now. He sat in a two-person-wide sofa and placed his feet on the short wooden set piece in front of him. He looked approvingly at the far wall, which was decorated with beautiful Chinese calligraphy that was hundreds of years old, as well as columns of traditional Chinese lanterns.

I admire the artists who make this calligraphy as such a beautiful art form, he thought.

After a few seconds, Yao thought somberly, *Alright. Time for some tea and a moment to gather my thoughts.*

The foreign minister rose to his feet and entered the teahouse's main room, which was easily the most festive room he'd yet seen in the lodge. Seven rounded tables were placed at regular intervals, each surrounded by five stools that mirrored the table's shape and style. In the space between the tables, red blimp-like spheres hung from the ceiling, on which hung, in turn, yellow cylinders. Both the red spheres and the yellow cylinders were made of fine paper, which Yao found quite pleasing.

"Excuse me, Foreign Minister," a young, lively voice said.

Yao turned to his right to find a triplet of women in staff uniform, all smiling pleasantly. "Hello to you all. I was hoping to sit down and enjoy some tea by myself."

"My name is Fen," the same woman said. "For all you've done for the Chinese people, we'd be honored to perform a tea ceremony for you."

Hearing that, Yao stood just a little taller. "Yes, that sounds lovely. Thank you."

"Take a seat, and we will return shortly."

Yao obliged. After a minute or so, the three women returned with a full tea set: a teapot, a cup bracket of teacups, a tea strainer, a kettle, water, a tea bowl, tea leaves, a tray, a fragrance smelling cup, and a tea leaf holder. Right in front of him, they rinsed the teapot and the teacups, since preheating helped to fully release the fragrance of the tea. Then they used tea chopsticks to insert tea leaves into the teapot. They poured hot water from the kettle into the teapot, only to pour out the water of the first brew into the empty container a few moments later. Yao knew that this was done to remove dust and other impurities from the tea leaves.

As Yao watched the tea ceremony, his stress over the failed negotiations abated, and his mind wandered introspectively.

Shanghai was a beautiful city to be born into. It has changed a lot, but even when I was a child, I marveled at its architecture. Father would show me the Shikumen, the folk houses of the city. And I remember visiting Tianzifang when it was merely a factory area. Now, it's a great enclave for tourists and arts and crafts, full of creative art galleries.

As a child, losing Father turned my world upside down. The damn Americans had killed him in the Korean War. But Father's heroism did not go unnoticed by Chairman Mao, who invited my maternal grandmother, Ju, to visit him in Zhongnanhai. Mao's son, too, was lost during the war. It was April of 1953, and I was only five years old.

Mao and my grandmother tightly held hands, bonding as only bereaved parents could.

"You have lost a son, as have I," Mao had said to her. "Their sacrifice was glorious. As their parents, we share in their glory."

He told us what a great man Father was and then gave my grandmother a poem that he'd written about the loss of his son.

The poem was passed on to me in 1965, when I was seventeen years old. It was only then that my grandmother told me about her meeting with Chairman Mao so many years ago. Just a year later, in 1966, my grandmother passed away.

As soon as I read the poem, I was enthralled, and I found more and more of Mao's poetry. To this day, I can recite every one of his poems. My interested in poetry only grew as I came of age. I even delved into calligraphy and painting, both of which have been foundations of Chinese artistic culture since ancient times.

Reading poetry and practicing calligraphy and painting have been my hobbies ever since I was a teenager. They are especially helpful when I am in need of some soul-searching. And I have kept Mao's original poem to this day, as an honorary gesture both to Mao and to Father.

The young lady refilled the teapot with hot water and lidded the pot. Yao closed his eyes as the tantalizing aroma of the tea filled his nostrils. It was producing exactly the effect that Yao had sought—a tranquil state of mind.

To this day, I treasure Mao's poem. After all, he is rightly regarded as one of the greatest poets in China's history, in addition to being known as the founder of the Communist Party of China. Few living Chinese can claim to own a piece of art created by our late, great leader.

Fen poured the tea into the tea bowl and then covered it with a tight seal. She then poured the tea into two small tea cups.

"Would you like us to leave the accoutrements on the table for you, Foreign Minister? We are happy to accommodate you however you wish."

Yao smiled and nodded. "Yes, please. Thank you."

The foreign minister watched as the young women walked away, remembering what it was like to be so young. Then he thought of his own time as a man in his early twenties.

I enjoyed my time at Beijing University. I majored in history, because I've always felt a bond with all of the great Chinese men and women who have come before me. But I knew that ignoring the rest of world history would have been a mistake, so I studied the history of the West, too. Part of those studies included learning Russian, English, and French.

But my university experience was not only textbooks. I met my wife, Zhao, during our introductory history class of freshman year. We fell in love so quickly that it scared me. Zhao was so beautiful, and more than my intellectual match. But she was always so much stronger than me, and she was my best friend and lover until her dying breath.

After graduation, I was invited to study in Russia for a year as part of a postgraduate program for gifted students. I couldn't bear to be apart from Zhao, so we quickly married—it was the only way that her dad would allow her to join me in Russia. Our time in Moscow turned out to be more momentous than either of us had anticipated, as Zhao gave birth to our daughter there. Of course, Ai would be our only child. The One Child Policy forbade us from having more.

From the moment I first saw my little Ai, I fell in love. While I was already headed in the direction of public service, at that moment I made an explicit promise to myself that I'd make China a better place for my daughter.

Yao brought his teacup to his nose, enjoyed a slow whiff, and took his first sip. He leaned back in his chair as the green tea made its way through his system.

I learned a lot during my time in the Soviet Union. Everywhere, there were long lines at stores. Like everyone else in Russia, I'd get in line and purchase goods, but they didn't always have what I wanted. There was a mess of shortages. All goods were rationed, so we could only purchase a limited amount of any good. Since the government forbade anyone from purchasing an arbitrary amount of anything, we were forced to trade with other people in the black market. There was a hunger in the people's eyes, both literally and figuratively. And so, when the U.S.S.R. fell, I was not surprised. I witnessed the very problems that would cause the empire's eventual disintegration.

When I returned to my native lands, I was recruited to the diplomatic core, which I accepted delightedly. The government quickly assigned me to be a diplomat to Bosnia. My wife was not pleased with the assignment, but I told her that I made a vow to make the world safe for our daughter.

Soon after I arrived in Bosnia, a terrible ethnic war erupted. The Bosnian War lasted from 1992 to 1995, and I was unfortunate enough to be there during the armed conflict. Early in 1992, Muslims, Croats, and Serbs had begun fighting each other. Around that time and following the breakup of Yugoslavia, the United States and the European Economic Community recognized Bosnia as an independent nation. I remember a Serb telling me that a single wedding was the first scene of violence that launched the entire war. Whether apocryphal or not, the country became awash with blood. Only a month after the war began, the Sijekovac killings of Serbs occurred in March, and the Bijelijina massacre of Bosniaks happened a week after that. Neighbor killed neighbor for days, weeks, months.

It was dangerous to be there. I was terrified that I'd never see my family again, but my hosts protected me. I convinced our ambassador to help save many of those who could have been slaughtered by housing them in the Chinese embassy. I've always held that innocent people do not deserve to die in war—'collateral damage' is morally unacceptable. I had learned about Japan's rape of Nanjing in school, during which hundreds of thousands of innocent Chinese were murdered. I would not allow such a tragedy to happen under my watch, and I'm proud to say that we were successful.

Yao took another sip of his tea, which was now only lukewarm. His eyes wandered around the room, and he noticed that even the staff was nowhere to be found.

Is it that obvious that I want to be left alone? I hope I wasn't rude to those women.

Yao's eyes fell back on his teacup, now nearly empty.

I went on to hold many other diplomatic posts after my time in Bosnia. I was ambassador to Russia for a time, which was fun for me. I had come to appreciate the people of the country for their culture: they were a hardened people. Gritty. They knew what they wanted and were not afraid to tell you.

Later, I was ambassador to the United States. That was when I first met Secretary Bryers. Admittedly, we spoke with each other only briefly, and always during meetings. But I knew arrogance when I encountered it. He was typical of the American ethos that I had become all too familiar with: entitled, self-centered, and morally righteous. I admit that, in those respects, he was nothing extraordinary. But Bryers, more than other Americans that I had met, thirsted for publicity. It was disgusting. My briefing papers on him included so many articles that he was in, or his television appearances. It was unprofessional, immature, and tasteless.

Finally, I became closer to fulfilling my promise to my wife when I became ambassador to the United Nations in New York. We loved New York City. During this time, I received word from my superiors that Bill Bryers was to be nominated for secretary-general before the United Nations. They told me to oppose his nomination and vote him down. They didn't give me a reason, but I knew that they did not want America taking over the United Nations. Frankly, I agreed with them. But more than that, I never would have voted for Bryers. He lacked the character necessary for such a role.

Bryers confronted me about my vote only once. I could see his anger, but he kept it in check. I admit, I was rude to him—I barely gave him the time of day and hardly said a word. Before this week, that was the last time I'd spoken to him.

Two years later, I was honored to be chosen as the next minister of foreign affairs. Since then, I have been a man of my duties. I have honored the promise to my wife, even after my wife left this world. And finally, I was set to retire … until the latest tragedy in the South China Sea.

Yao finished his tea and rose to his feet. *The negotiations may have failed,* he thought, his hands tightening into fists, *but this conflict between China and the United States will not end until China is respected for the global superpower that she is.*

SEVENTEEN
★★★
CHAPTER

B
ill left his room and went to the hotel bar by the lobby. He found a corner table to be by himself.

"I'll have a Budweiser, please," Bill said to the well-dressed bartender.

"I have something much better," the bartender replied. "Qingdao beer."

"Okay. I'll try it."

The man began to smile at Bill, but as he saw the secretary of state's heavy expression, the bartender simply nodded wordlessly.

"Thanks," Bill muttered.

Everything went to hell, he thought to himself. *Between my son-in-law and the failed negotiations, I can't think of a worse day in recent memory.*

The bartender returned to give Bill his glass of beer. Bill paid and added a generous tip, since he knew the energy he was giving off and felt bad about it. Bill felt sick, dejected, and hopeless. He thought that he had failed his country.

Come on, don't wallow, he thought to himself. Then he took a deep swig followed by a heavy breath. "Wow, that's good," he whispered. "That's one good thing that happened today."

Memories of his deceased son-in-law took Bill further into the past. *I loved my time at Yale University. I was so grateful to have been accepted by the prestigious Ivy League institution in New Haven, Connecticut. It has a long history of excellent research and producing famous graduates.*

I had so many friends there. I was even elected president of my freshman class. Eventually, I was invited to the Skull and Bones secret society. I'm proud to say that many previous American presidents were members of the society.

I majored in political science, of course. I was honored to have met some of the most famous professors of politics and related subjects on the planet. In our private conversations, I learned more than I ever did in the classroom. One professor in particular, Dr. Roberts, kindly removed the utopian delusions I'd held in my youth about politics. Before I met him, I thought that all political issues could be resolved if only we got everyone to agree on the facts. Then, 'of course' the solution would be obvious to everyone. But no. Dr. Roberts explained to me that every political issue is far more complicated than that. Even if everyone agreed on the facts, people would always disagree about how to interpret the facts, about economics, and about moral values. So politics was more of an art than a science, he said.

I dated a lot in college, but I didn't have a serious girlfriend until my senior year, when I met my now wife. I saw her sitting alone at the café that I frequented on campus. Sloan was reading a history book that I'd read, and I thought she was cute, so I tried to impress her by telling her my thoughts about the book. She didn't seem impressed, but she let me buy her a cup of coffee, anyway. And we talked for hours. I knew I wanted to marry her by the end of the day.

Bill looked at the alcohol collection behind the bar. He saw plenty of classic American liquors, but there were also many Chinese beverages that he'd seen in the past. He smiled mirthlessly. *They tried to keep us all happy. I guess a mixed bar wasn't enough to make that happen.*

All of the alcohol triggered Bill's memories of his time in Washington, D.C., as a young man. *During the summer before my senior year at Yale, I interned at Congress for one of Dad's colleagues. I loved Capitol Hill—the buildings, the people, the culture ... all of it. There, I worked in the Cannon House Office Building, which is sometimes called the "Old House Office Building." It's about one hundred years old. Most people don't know that the first congressional office buildings were built only at the dawn of the twentieth century in order to reduce the overcrowding that had begun to plague the Capitol. Before the construction of these buildings, anyone who needed office space had to rent or borrow committee rooms elsewhere in the Capitol. Whenever I think back to this bit of history, I always find it rather amusing—I can't help but chuckle at images of the most important members of our society in such undignified state of affairs. Fortunately, Congress solved the problem in 1901, when they authorized Edward Clark, architect of the Capitol, to oversee the construction of official office buildings.*

Just a week into my internship, I knew that I wanted to somehow work in or with Congress and make a difference. I spent many nights attending parties thrown by renowned associations, trade groups, lobbyists, embassies, and think tanks. The food was always delicious, and back then, I was always hungry. Members of Congress and their staff often attended, which always made my heart skip a beat. I loved meeting so many powerful people at these parties, but once they heard my last name, they'd ask me if I was related to Dad. Every time, I'd think, 'I've accomplished things, too, you know.' But I'd never say it.

"Are you doing okay?" the bartender asked Bill.

Bill took another swig of his beer and nodded at the worker. "Yeah, thanks. Bring another one when you have a chance. Thank you."

As the bartender went to fetch the secretary of state another beer, Bill continued to distract himself with his own history. *I did what Dad advised. Every time I met someone new in Washington, I collected their business cards and wrote notes on the back of them as soon as I returned to my apartment: how I met the person, and what we talked about. I also noted if they were donors to political campaigns, in case I ever wanted to run for Congress.*

I ended up serving in the military after college. I figured that it'd be a great way to launch a career in Washington later on, plus I'd get to serve my country in the meantime. I wound up in Iraq during the Gulf War. The United States decided to respond to Iraq's imperialistic attack on Kuwait. I kept up with the politics of the situation to the best of my ability. The Gulf War was comprised of two operations: Operation Desert Shield and Operation Desert Storm. Leading up to the war, I had thought that the international sanctions imposed on Iraq would have stopped the Iraqis from continuing their invasion of Kuwait. I was so young, so naïve. I learned that evil actors cannot always be tempered by merely peaceful resistance. Sometimes—tragically—force is required.

I'm proud of my Bronze Star that I earned for bravery in Iraq. I'd led a platoon on a very dangerous mission to rescue fellow soldiers who were trapped behind enemy lines. As we escaped, I was shot in the shoulder.

Bill's eyes began to water, and the half-empty glass of beer became blurry. *My friend Tim Stupple died that day. I'd only known him for a year, but war brings people closer than anything else does. He was always so jovial. I remember crying as I wrote a letter to his parents, telling them about their son's fate. And I remember my righteous anger about his life being wasted.*

After the war, I flew to Kansas to see Tim's parents to show my respects for their loss. They had a lovely little farm. It was just missing a strapping young man. I felt the sad emptiness in their company, but they were grateful to hear stories about Tim. I knew then that I had to prevent this from happening again. I wasn't so naïve that I thought I could bring about world peace, but I knew that I could help to end conflicts between nations. It was to be my duty for the rest of my life.

After a few minutes of mental wandering, Bill recalled his years after service. *I went to law school at Yale. I would practically memorize lists of all of the United States presidents, secretaries of state, and Supreme Court justices who had also graduated from Yale Law School: Gerald Ford, Bill Clinton, Clarence Thomas, and Sonia Sotomayor. I never cared if I agreed with them politically or not. Just to have walked where they walked, and ate where they ate, felt magical to me.*

Upon graduation, I worked for a prestigious law firm until I ran for Congress in Dad's old district and won.

But I was far from finished. I landed a seat on the foreign relations committee and quickly became a leader on most foreign policy topics. I'd been preparing my entire life for this moment. Every career choice I'd made, every book I'd read—it all culminated with this. I wound up being asked to go on cable television shows quite frequently, so that I could give my thoughts on the latest international issues. I'd been keeping up with current events around the world for decades by that point. I became a household name, a nationally recognized congressman.

After years of dating, I finally married Sloan, and we had two beautiful daughters in short order. Gabrielle and Samantha mean everything to me. I'd been blessed with a wonderful family. After work, I'd always take the girls to the playground. We'd climb and swing and run around. I'd pretend to be a monster and scream and chase them. I felt so alive.

When a Senate seat opened up, I ran and, to my surprise, I won. After another decade of working my tail off to serve the American people, I gained seniority and became Chairman of Foreign Relations in the Senate. I led this standing committee of the Senate, responsible for leading foreign policy legislation and debate in the Senate. We were responsible for treaties, America's foreign aid efforts, weapons sales to allies, and confirmation hearings for various positions in the Department of State.

In this role, I made many powerful friends around the world. I acquired a reputation for settling disputes between world leaders. I still can't believe how many peace negotiations I've been a part of. I've prevented wars in the Middle East, Latin America, and Africa. I haven't won it, but I've been nominated for a Nobel Peace Prize. I thought of Tim Stupple so often during this period of my life. I was finally doing what I'd set out to do. God, what a life I've lived. I'm so grateful.

Bill's hands turned to fists as a flare of frustration overtook him. *I became so respected worldwide that I found myself in contention for the role of secretary-general of the United Nations. It was my dream job, of course. The secretary-general is the chief administration officer of the United Nations and head of the United Nations Secretariat, which is the executive arm of the United Nations. I've always maintained a realistic perspective on myself—at least, I think I have. And I knew that I was ready for this job, this crown achievement. But China and Russia led an effort to vote against me. And Yao headed that effort. He won the day.*

But I refused to let Yao keep me down. I was later nominated by the president to be his secretary of state. The Senate voted me in, and here I am. I've always succeeded in my efforts as secretary of state ...

Until now.

"Would you like another beer, Secretary?"

Bill looked up. He had been so immersed in his thoughts that he hadn't noticed the empty glasses of beer and water in front of him. "Oh, yes, thank you."

"We are closing up soon, but take your time. Just don't go outside anytime soon."

Bill frowned. "What do you mean?"

"The clouds are looking heavy, like they'll burst any second. And at this temperature, it could snow."

A snowstorm? Bill thought. *I don't believe it. My day can't get any worse. We have a flight in the morning.*

There's no way that can happen. I want to see my family. And I'll be damned if I have to live like a prisoner in this lodge, stuck with those arrogant Chinese delegates.

Fingers crossed.

EIGHTEEN
★★★
CHAPTER

South China Sea

"**G**o ahead and launch half of our fighter jets," the admiral said to the captain in the U.S. aircraft carrier. "We need to give air cover protection to our fleet. And send communications to the Chinese that if their ships or aircrafts approach our fleet, they will be destroyed without warning. Make sure you confirm that the Chinese have received this message."

Bill's alarm went off at the crack of dawn. He rolled over, shut it off, and jumped out of bed.

Wondering whether or not he needed to wear a coat to the airport, he walked over to his room's window and peered outside.

Snow covered everything, piled high enough to smother many of the beautiful features he had seen only yesterday. And it continued to fall in a torrent of wind and thick white droplets.

"Oh, no, no, no."

Before he could reach his phone to call the Air Force Two pilot who was sent to retrieve him, someone knocked on his door.

"One second, please!" he called.

After quickly throwing on a white undershirt and a pair of dark jeans, Bill opened the door to find Ashley, one of his staffers. She was dressed in a casual blouse and a pair of black heels.

Not exactly flight attire, Bill thought with concern.

"Good morning, Ashley. Please, come in."

Bill turned the lights on and sat on his bed, letting Ashley take the chair.

"Please don't say what I think you're going to say," Bill muttered.

Ashley pursed her lips and squirmed. "Ah, yes, Secretary. Our flight has been canceled due to an unexpected blizzard. We are to remain at the lodge for the foreseeable future."

Bill cursed under his breath. "And the Chinese?"

"We're all stuck here," Ashley answered.

"Right," Bill said through his teeth. "I suppose we'll all just … hang out."

Bill saw that Ashley still had something to say, but she was holding back. "Ashley? Please, speak up."

"We highly recommend that you convene with Sheng," she said nervously. "It's proper diplomatic protocol."

Bill put his hand to his forehead. "I feel like God is playing a joke on me. Yeah, okay. It's the right thing to do."

Ashley smiled in relief. "Great. Sheng is being told the same as we speak. I can come back to show you the way to the private dining room, once you're dressed. You'll be meeting at eight o'clock."

Bill blinked. He hadn't expected to be meeting with Sheng so immediately. *Might as well rip off the bandage.*

"Alright. I'll meet you outside my room in a couple of hours. Thank you, Ashley."

Bill chose to spend some time writing a letter to his in-laws, who had only just lost their son on the ship. As he wrote, his heart melted at the thought of his poor daughter and of his grandkids who would grow up without their dad.

When the time came, he rose to his feet and mentally prepared himself for his meeting with Sheng. As Bill brushed his teeth and changed into his suit, he was filled with a strange cocktail of emotions—confusion, anxiety, and guilt. Only minutes ago, he had thought that he would be returning to his country today. And now, he was trapped with people whom he had hoped he would never see again.

I need to tell my wife, he thought after he finished putting on his suit.

The call was painful. He told his wife everything—their failure to arrive at a diplomatic solution, and now his failure to come home. And they commiserated over their daughter's newfound status as a widow. But she was nothing but understanding, as she always was.

"I will be back soon," he promised her, and hung up the phone.

Finally, he opened the door to meet a patiently waiting Ashley.

"Shall we?" he asked teasingly.

Ashley nodded and silently led Bill to the dining room. The door was wooden, decorated with imprints of classic Chinese iconography, and had no windows into which Bill could see the inside.

"Good luck, Secretary."

Bill nodded at Ashley. "Thank you. Here goes nothing."

The secretary of state opened the door to find a single, long table that hosted three exquisite Chinese dishes scattered across it. The steam coming from the breakfast foods made Bill's mouth water. He glanced out through the room's windows to see the Great Wall covered in snow. It reminded him of something he'd seen in a fantasy film.

"It's beautiful, isn't it?"

Bill turned to find Yao, sitting so still by the middle of the table that he had not registered on Bill's radar. He was dressed as professionally as he was yesterday, but Bill thought that he looked tired.

"Yes, it is. The Great Wall is a symbol of China's unification since the Qin Dynasty."

Yao gestured for Bill to take a seat across from him. Bill obliged and glanced at the empty plate in front of him.

"I suspect this will go better if we fill our bellies," Sheng said.

Bill nodded, eager for any excuse to cut through the tense awkwardness. "I'll follow your lead."

Yao smiled dryly and poured a handful of steamed stuffed buns onto his plate. He then offered some to Bill, who nodded in approval.

They began eating, with only the howls of the blizzard breaking the silence.

After they finished, Sheng looked at Bill with an unreadable expression.

"Minister," Bill said softly. "I know I already said this, but I am sincerely sorry about your wife. My wife is my rock. I could not imagine life without her."

Sheng nodded slowly. "I appreciate that, Secretary. Truly. And I am sorry to hear of the tragic loss of your son-in-law."

Bill still felt tense, so he opted for a different direction. "Our respective nations have quite a complicated history, don't they?"

"Indeed. A long and checkered relationship. You colonized Shanghai in the middle of the nineteenth century. Perhaps ironic, given that your war over slavery would occur so soon after that."

Bill nearly scoffed, but he stopped himself. "To be fair, the British expressed more interest in Shanghai than we did."

"And yet you forged ahead, anyway," Sheng said with no emotion.

"We were allies in World War II," Bill said, intent on shifting to a more conciliatory chapter in history. "In 1940, when Japan signed the Tripartite Pact with Germany and Italy, our president, Roosevelt, helped the Chinese buy war supplies. And we imposed sanctions on Japan."

"You tried to negotiate with the Japanese," Sheng said accusingly.

"Yes, but it wasn't out of self-interest. We commanded Japan withdraw its forces from China."

"And you only declared war on Japan after they bombed Pearl Harbor."

Bill took a breath to conceal his frustration. "Our country enjoyed an abundance of pro-China messages at the time. One particular film series, *Why We Fight*, valorized the Chinese resistance of the Japanese imperialists. And Chiang Kai-shek was on the cover of *Time* magazine twice. The only reason our burgeoning alliance broke apart is because the communists won in your civil war."

"On that, we agree," Sheng said. "And so we became enemies once more. The Korean War was quite something. I remember that your president, Truman, did not initially wish to intervene."

Bill nodded. "But then we realized that South Korea's relationship with Japan was important to us in the fight against communism."

"So many atrocities," Sheng said sadly. "The South Korean president, Syngman Rhee, ordered mass slaughters of those who were suspected of being left wing. That Bodo League massacre resulted in anywhere from sixty thousand to two hundred thousand deaths. And the Americans are not innocent. Your troops murdered nearly three hundred refugees at No Gun Ri in South Korea, mostly women and children. You tortured Chinese prisoners of war. You cut off their limbs and coerced them into writing confession letters."

"Sixty-six percent of all American POWs in the Korean War died because of war crimes," Bill said defensively. "Most of your camps were situated close to the Korean-Chinese border, where they could have easily acquired food. And yet you intentionally starved many of your prisoners so that they would take communist ideology onboard. War is messy, Minister. There is plenty of blood on all of our hands. The question is, how do we move forward?"

Sheng poured himself a cup of tea and took a long sip before responding. "You are right. Please forgive my mood."

Bill raised an open hand. "Not a problem."

"I must admit, relations between our nations have seen worse days. Following the September 11th attacks on your World Trade Center, we did begin to mend fences."

Bill smiled lightly. "I recall. Many of your institutions and private citizens offered their condolences at the time."

"And we sympathized with your War on Terror," Sheng replied. "The PRC supported your efforts in Afghanistan, and we gave one hundred and fifty million dollars to the Afghan reconstruction project when the Taliban was routed. Our governments engaged in fruitful conversations about counterterrorism."

"I remember," Bill said calmly. "Between you and me, I suspect that Chinese-U.S. relations improved after 9/11 because it became implausible that you were our most serious security risk. Clearly that was coming from the Middle East, not the Far East."

Sheng smirked. "I appreciate your honesty. To balance the scales, let me tell you this: at the time, our government was worried that your war on terrorism would actually result in an anti-PRC campaign from the United States. You were, after all, setting up military positions in Uzbekistan and Tajikistan. But then, as you struggled in Iraq, and as you showed a desire to work *with* us, much of our initial anxiety abated."

Bill helped himself to another dumpling.

Sheng chuckled. "You like those, don't you?"

Bill swallowed and said, "I'm enjoying those parts of China that present themselves to me. It's not every day that you're inside of a blizzard with the Great Wall as your backdrop. I'm just trying to immerse myself in the experience."

Sheng grinned, and Bill was relieved that the Chinese diplomat appreciated the joke. "Indeed. Indeed."

"Look, Minister. It's clear that you and I have different worldviews. But I feel that I have failed my country—our summit resulted in nothing."

"I feel the same way," Sheng said with a shrug. "But there is always hope. I'm not sure how much I believe in fate, but this blizzard is quite coincidental timing." He suddenly looked above Bill, as if he was recalling a distant memory. "You mentioned my wife. If she is in heaven, I sometimes worry that she has forgotten me. There is an old Chinese myth that says, when one has died and begun travelling on the road to rebirth, one crosses a bridge and drinks the soup of forgetfulness. After drinking the soup, one would forget everything that happened and everyone one knows in one's past life. Only then is one ready to be incarnated." Sheng's eyes filled with tears. "After that, you drink a soup and forget all of your memories. Everything you knew. Everyone you ... you loved ..."

Bill did not know what to say. "I'm sorry, Sheng."

Sheng wiped his eyes. "I have made my peace. If the myth is true, then she has long ago crossed over that bridge and been reborn. And while I may be gone from her spirit, she still lives in me. You said that your wife is your rock. Mine is, too. And I will never lose hope so long as she is inside of me."

Even Bill's heartstrings were pulled. "So where do we go from here?"

Sheng took another sip from his tea. "For all intents and purposes, we are the only people in the world. It is a good time to sit, eat, and think."

Sheng's emotional oration caused Bill to think about his own family. After a long pause, he said, "All of these issues—diplomacy, geopolitics, international war—my grandfather lived such a simpler life, and yet I respect him more than almost anyone."

Sheng leaned forward, interested if only because of the cordial tone that Bill took. "Oh?"

"His life was one of blood, sweat, and tears. He was a farmer."

Sheng opened his mouth in surprise. "My grandfather was a farmer, too!"

"You don't say? So you know exactly what I mean."

Sheng nodded. "He never stopped working until the day he died."

Bill looked out once again at the magnificent Great Wall of China. "Do you think they ever took a moment to stop and smell the roses? I bet not, busy as they were tilling the field. I remember his farm, deep in my bones. The scents, the sights, the sounds—I had wonderful childhood experiences from summers on the farm. I'd run through his fields and roll in the hay without a care in the world."

"Today the U.S. farms are a major source of food for China."

Bill suddenly felt energized. Merely minutes ago, he felt that he had been walking on eggshells with Sheng, but now, it was as if this was their first meeting without their troubled past looming in their minds.

Maybe Sheng is right. Maybe there is hope, after all.

NINETEEN
★★★
CHAPTER

U nited States National Security Advisor John Bannister rose from his daily push-up routine and muttered a curse under his breath.

This snowstorm complicates things, he thought in frustration. *Diplomacy had failed. But now, maybe Yao and Bill have a second chance. And they are quite talented, doves though they might be. But I'm not finished yet, either.*

We must fight China now, before they get too strong.

A few hours earlier, Bannister had been informed that the president wanted to speak with him at eleven in the morning, a time that was quickly approaching. As the security advisor prepared to hop in the shower, the magnitude of his goals suddenly dawned on him, and his thoughts drifted into nostalgia.

I've become so powerful, he thought proudly as he turned the shower on. *I've certainly made more of myself than my father ...*

As Bannister began scrubbing the sweat off himself in a cold shower, his thoughts drifted even further into the past. *I remember my parents moving us to the New York suburbs when I was very young. We'd been living in a small apartment in the Bronx. Years later, Mom told me that crime had become too rampant for us to stay there. Once she got a new job in banking, we could afford to move to Westchester, where the air was cleaner and the people were more lawful. Of course, that didn't stop me from living like an animal. I ran around town causing all kinds of chaos. I've always loved the thrill of danger—my friends and I would start fires, smoke who-knows-what, and skip school whenever we felt like it. And I loved every minute of it.*

But I always felt different from my friends. While they were into sports, I was into the U.S. military. I'd play in my room for hours on end with toy soldiers. I'd make up battles, create tons of different scenarios, and play them out in interesting ways. My parents would watch television after dinner, and I'd beg them to watch war movies and documentaries about war.

I remember learning about the CIA and that it was founded on September 18th, 1947—a date I remember as indelibly as my own birthday. Even some Americans despise the CIA, but they are ignorant. They don't realize what the organization has had to deal with and the victories that it's helped to usher in. We owe our post-World War II world dominance largely to them.

My passion for geopolitics only grew with age, which is why I was so ashamed to learn about my father's cowardice in his youth. Apparently, he was of age during World War II, but he was a 'conscientious objector'—a euphemism for 'coward.' Dad ended up serving the country by doing laundry at military training camps. Pathetic.

By the time I was a teenager, I was living a double life. At home, I was still playing war games and reading all the books I could get my hands on about military history, geopolitics, and the nature of war. And outside of the house, I continued to run wild with my friends. I was arrested twice for theft—once for a condom, and once for a lighter. I don't smoke anymore, but even back then, I loved women. The judge warned me that one more act of theft would land me in juvenile detention. I argued with my parents that night, and, to my delighted surprise, we came to a common solution—they'd send me to military school. The dream!

It was everything I thought it would be and then some. My roommate, Mike, became a close friend of mine. It was magical, having a friend who actually shared my interests. He ended up becoming the current president of the United States. While I was just a teenager, God had blessed me with the opportunity of a lifetime, although I couldn't have known that at the time. But the chess pieces had been set in place . . .

New York Military School is located in the beautiful Catskills, New York. The Catskills are famous for its resorts and was extremely popular with New Yorkers before air travel became affordable for the middle and upper classes. It was also a training ground for tons of comedians. Go figure, right? I've never been into comedy, myself. Too many real villains out there for me to enjoy a chuckle.

Bannister finished showering and dried himself off. He looked at himself in the mirror, impressed at the build he'd maintained, even at his age. *I don't quite look as good as I did when I went to Harvard, but good enough.*

An embarrassing memory hit him out of nowhere. *But despite my love of the military, despite my trajectory, I failed to put my money where my mouth was. I was of age during the Vietnam War. But ... I was scared. I convinced a doctor who was against the war to fake a medical diagnosis for me, so that I could avoid the draft. It was the greatest mistake of my life.*

But I'll make up for it. The United States military is the greatest force in the world. We are humanity's police, as we should be. Of the nearly two hundred countries on earth, we have a military presence in about one hundred and fifty of them. Various treaties bind us to protect nearly seventy countries if they are attacked. And we often get something in return for our protection. We have nearly fifty thousand military personnel in Japan, and we enjoy nearly two hundred billion dollars' worth of trade with the country. In the Middle East, we protect many of the splintered tribes, and we maintain relations with those who sell us oil and gas. We are the greatest country in the history of the world.

Bannister returned to his bedroom and picked out his clothing for the day. He chose his most professional outfit, even though his call with the president was audio only. He always dressed for the occasion.

Finally, he picked up the phone. "Yes, this is Bannister," he said to the White House staff member on the other line. "The president is expecting my call."

"One moment, please."

Bannister cracked his knuckles in anticipation as he waited. He knew what he had to do, and he was utterly certain that he was righteous.

"John," the president said after a minute. "I'm sorry about the circumstances."

"Thank you, Mr. President," Bannister said politely. "But you know what? This might not be so bad. From here, things could go either way: worse or better. But things certainly won't stay the same."

The president laughed lightly through the phone. "You're not usually one for riddles. What's your mind?"

"I'm sure you've already been told that diplomacy has failed. Their foreign minister butted heads with Bill. Reached an impasse."

"But now that everyone is stuck in the same place, maybe they can work it out."

Bannister frowned. "Or … what happens here can bring us closer to war."

"You've hinted at this path before, John," the president said slowly. "Why are you so adamant about going to war with China? I'm not asking dismissively. You know I value your opinion, though I still strongly prefer peace."

"Because we can take them," Bannister growled. "But the time to do it is now. In ten years, they'll have a navy so powerful that we might not be able to overpower them. But as of now, *we* are the world's superpower. Not them."

"Hmm. But surely a fight is not inevitable?"

Bannister scoffed. "Yeah, it is. War is always waiting, Mr. President. We will clash with China, one way or another. They show no signs of slowing down their military expansion. The only question is, will we fight them when we're stronger than they are, or will we let the opportunity pass us by?"

"It would mean a lot of dead bodies, John. In the age of social media, a politician's career can be ruined by a single video of bloodshed. I'm not sure I want that."

"Respectfully, you're not thinking this through. Of course war will result in casualties. But if we can convince the American people that the Chinese are the bad guys, a mainstream media and social media campaign here and there won't curb the people's lust for war."

"Say I agree with you. I still can't just unleash the American military on China right now. It would be too egregious in the eyes of the international community. But you already know that, so what's your big idea?"

Bannister smiled mirthlessly. "My sources have been keeping me up-to-date on the South China Sea. Things are getting tense over there. The Chinese and our own soldiers have engaged with their respective allies. This is bigger than just our enmity with China. This is becoming the moment when the world sees who the real global hegemon is. We just need a little push, and we'll have war." He looked out his room's window at the blizzard that had trapped him in the lodge. "I can be that push. Hell, more diplomacy might be exactly what we need."

"I'm sorry, John, I'm confused."

"It's best if I don't say more, Mr. President. But I have to ask: are you willing to wage war with the Chinese? Your answer will determine my next actions. You know that wartime presidents get a big boost in popularity, and the midterm congressional elections are coming soon. This would carry our party to victory."

There was a long pause. Bannister held his breath, and he could hear the rapid beating of his heart.

"Yes."

The security advisor nodded. "Okay, Mr. President."

"Is there anything else you'd like to share? Protests have been exploding across the country, and I need to tend to them. Some citizens clamoring for peace, others pounding the war drums. You can imagine."

"I certainly can," Bannister said, still smiling like a kid in a candy shop. "I'm glad we spoke. Go take care of business on your end, and I'll do the same."

"Stay safe, John."

They both hung up, and Bannister took a moment to assess the situation. While he had little patience and a short temper, when he was alone, he was adept at planning, thinking through his actions, and predicting the downstream consequences of his decisions.

He picked up the phone and made another call. "Hey. It's me. Come to my room. We need to talk."

After several minutes, there was a knock on the door. Bannister opened it to see Josh standing nervously in sweatpants and a loose, long-sleeved shirt. The security advisor pulled him inside and closed the door.

"Hey," Josh began, "I—"

"You still have the envelope?" Bannister interrupted. "It's time."

Josh swallowed. "Uh, yeah, but—"

"No buts. You need to get that black dot onto Guo's clothing. The athletic one who doesn't wear any makeup. She's their expert on American history."

"How do you expect me to do that?"

"Not my problem. But get it done."

Josh nervously rubbed his hands together. "Mr. Bannister ..."

"Don't tell me you're getting cold feet. Literally, don't say it. You don't have a choice."

While Bannister stared at Josh, Josh looked at the ground. "I'm not sure I thought this through ..."

"Listen to me, boy. I will do more than end your career. I will burn you so hard that your entire family will bow their heads in shame for the next century. And you know I'm good for it. So pick your head up and do as I say."

Finally, Josh met Bannister's hard, fiery eyes. "By when?"

"Today."

Josh nodded. "Okay."

As he walked past Bannister towards the door, the security advisor put a strong arm out and stopped Josh. "One more thing. You're the assistant secretary of state. And you still have the Dictaphone. Get Bill on record saying ... unflattering words about the Chinese. Or Yao in particular. I don't care. Just make sure it's bad."

"You want that done today, too?"

Bannister cocked his head and thought about it. "This can't take you more than a day. Keep me in the loop. This is your chance, Josh. Honor or shame. It's your choice."

"Yes, sir."

Bannister let him go.

The security advisor stood alone, breathing slowly and contemplating his next move.

TWENTY
★★★
CHAPTER

One Year Earlier

Washington, D.C.

Bannister, close friend and advisor to the president, had asked the young and newly appointed assistant secretary of state to lunch at the prestigious Metropolitan Club.

Josh was nervous.

Bannister had arrived early and was already sitting at the table when Josh arrived.

"Good to meet you, sir," Josh said seriously.

Bannister did not shake his hand. "This club is over one hundred and fifty years old. Many long-term political friendships started here. This place is beautiful, and I love the power it represents. The president and I often dine at this very table."

"I like it here, too," Josh said subserviently.

"You know I got you your job."

Josh raised his eyebrows in surprise. "Um, you did? Well, thank you! But why?"

Bannister did not answer.

After a few minutes of silently reviewing the menu, Bannister said, "Joshy boy, let me ask you this. Who is the greatest threat to the United States?"

Josh swallowed and looked back into Bannister's friendly but intense eyes. "It's gotta be Middle Eastern terrorists. 9/11 was only the beginning. There are so many disparate terrorist organizations, it's like fighting a hydra. And they hate us."

Bannister reached over and patted Josh on the leg. "I like you, Josh. But with all due respect, they're no longer the enemy. I grant that there are many, many dangerous actors in that part of the world, but they have little *power* compared to others."

Josh frowned. "What do you mean?"

Steaks arrived, even before Josh had a chance to look at the menu. Bannister took a greedy bite of his and took his time before responding. "I ordered for both of us. Eat, I insist. Now to answer your question: first of all, the United States is nearly entirely self-sufficient with respect to oil. Our ties to the Middle East are worthless at this point. More importantly, Russia and China have grown tremendously in recent years. And they hate the West at least as much as many Middle Eastern factions do. I understand the focus on terrorism, but we must move on to bigger fish in the sea."

Josh shook his head. "But … they haven't attacked Americans like the terrorists have."

"It's a new age, Joshy," Bannister said dramatically. "Physical assault isn't the only kind of attack. Surely you're familiar with the concept of an information war. The Russians and the Chinese have been engaged in one with the West for long enough. It's time we do something about it."

Josh glanced at his half-eaten steak before looking back up at Bannister, who now wore a more aggressive expression. "What did you have in mind?"

Bannister placed both hands on the table and closed his fists. "We need to take out China, in particular. I want to crush them before they grow even more powerful."

"What do you mean?"

Bannister narrowed his eyes. "You know exactly what I mean. We need to root them out, root and branch. We need to defeat them by any means necessary. You wrote as much in your own work."

"What?" Josh gasped. "I *never* suggested violent measures. Sir … this sounds wrong. I wrote in my publications and editorials that we need to find a way to defeat China economically. We should increase manufacturing, mine for precious minerals, and restrict trade before they become the largest economy in the world. I didn't mean that we need to defeat them militarily!"

Bannister paused for a long while. Josh squirmed in discomfort during the silence.

"Are you a coward, Josh?" Bannister asked quietly. "Like your dad?"

Josh's eyebrows went up and his heart raced. "Wh-what did you say?"

"Ah, there it is. I read your security file. I know that your father was discharged from the army for cowardice in battle. Wise of you to keep that to yourself."

"What is this?!" Josh yelled. "I'm nothing like my father. I haven't even spoken to him in years."

"Keep your voice down," Bannister said calmly. "Blood runs deep. And I know that he eventually became a successful businessman, only to go bankrupt."

"Why are you saying these things?" Josh asked. "What do you want from me?"

"I want to trade with you, Joshy," Bannister said quietly. "You see, I know you already think I'm dangerous. How do I know that? Because you lied."

Josh's hands were shaking. "N-no, I didn't lie!"

"Oh, yes, you did. You don't really believe that the Middle East harbors the most dangerous enemies of America. You came into this lunch knowing that I'm a hawk on China."

"I was sincerely excited to meet with you," Josh pleaded. "I thought maybe you'd offer to help my career. But …"

Bannister gestured towards Josh. "Go on, boy. Spit out the truth."

"But then you went right into foreign policy. And I don't want war with China. So y-yes, I lied. Are you happy?"

"I will be. You see, I'm actually glad that you lied to me today. I see how *good* you are at it. I'll need that talent in the near future. And by the way, I *am* making you a career offer. You must know that I have a personal relationship with the president. I can get you anything you want, any position you so desire."

For the first time during their meeting, Josh felt temptation. "I … I …"

Bannister waved an impatient hand. "I read your papers and lectures about China being the next great threat. I know that you already agree with me. Again, kudos for hiding it this entire time."

Josh gritted his teeth. "I didn't say that I want to *destroy* them!"

Bannister laughed. "So young, so naïve. Listen, boy, I expect to head to China sometime soon. The South China Sea is a powder keg. Something's gonna give. When that happens, the United States and China will send diplomats to try to keep the peace. I won't let that happen."

Josh swallowed nervously. "Why shouldn't I report you?"

"Because who would believe you? I am the president's friend. You would be fired. And I'd also make sure everyone in this city knows about your familial legacy, and your career will be finished. On the other hand, if you work with me, I can launch your career into the stratosphere."

Josh rose to his feet. "Why are you doing this?" he asked desperately. "Why do you need my help, anyway?"

Bannister pushed aside his finished plate but remained seated. "I care about the United States' position as world leader more than anything else in life. Maintaining its hegemony has been my life's work. I will not let it slip away, especially when I can do something about it.

"But I can't do this alone. I'll need help. When crisis does break out, I'm sure Bryers will be assigned to the diplomatic efforts. I will arrange it so that you continue to work with him, no matter what. I could use you."

Josh wiped his face. "This is crazy. You're asking me to make an impossible choice."

"Maybe I can arrange for you to be secretary of state one day." Finally, Bannister rose to his feet and stuck out his hand for Josh to shake. "I'll take your silence as a 'yes.'"

Josh stared at Bannister's open hand for a long while before finally making the decision to shake it.

TWENTY-ONE
★★★
CHAPTER

Spratley Islands, South China Sea, China

"Remember," General Yichen said to the handful of commanders before him, "if the American navy crosses into our territory in the South China Sea, you are ordered to fight."

They stood on a wooden platform where the South China Sea met the beach of their artificial island. The waters in front of them held a vast array of Chinese military infrastructure, much of it only a few years old: airstrips and hangers, anti-ship cruise missile systems, airships, radars, and naval ships.

"What if they don't back down?" one of the commanders asked.

"They will," Yichen said confidently. "They can't afford a war with us."

"What about our allies? I don't see them anywhere."

"Don't worry so much, Zimo. Russia will come at a moment's notice." Yichen put a strong hand on his subordinate's shoulder. "Russia has been prodding us to launch an attack on the Americans ever since we joined hands with them. But we are not stupid. We will act when it suits *us*. No one can control us."

"Last report said that the Americans are inching closer to our artificial islands in the South China Sea," another commander said. "How will we know when to attack?"

"There are many paths to the first strike," Yichen answered. "For example, if the Americans violate freedom of navigation as expressed in the 1982 United Nations Convention on the Law of the Sea, there will be hell to pay. We're all students of history. They must respect two hundred miles around these islands."

"Maybe you could tell us," Zimo said sheepishly, "in case some of us forgot?"

Yichen stared at Zimo with a humorless, daunting gaze. "Let me expound. The agreement established a legal framework for all maritime conduct across the globe. Rules about limits, navigation, exclusive economic zones, and settlement of disputes were laid out for all political regimes that signed the treaty. For our purposes, it is the treaty's words about territorial waters that I have in mind. It is written that a given coastal state is free to set laws and use whatever resources it can find in its territorial waters. Here is the key: vessels are allowed to pass through territorial waters by what is known as 'innocent passage.' This was defined as passage that is not 'prejudicial to the peace, good order, or security' of the coastal state."

"Aha!" Zimo exclaimed. "You think the Americans will break the peace!"

"Hold on, young man. *Military* craft is allowed what is called 'transit passage,' which means that they can effectively traverse waters with full intention to intimidate us. But I think there is a loophole we can exploit. We can suspend innocent passage in as many channels in the South China Sea as we want. We could thus prevent the Americans from moving freely around these parts. It's a bloodless strategy—we could win the war without firing a shot."

"I haven't heard of this before," another commander said. "How likely is it?"

Yichen shook his head. "I don't know yet, Lao. These measures take considerable time to pass, and everything is happening so fast in the South China Sea. But it's one option, and it will grow more attractive if and when the Americans enter disputed territory."

"Say that doesn't work," Lao said. "What then?"

"Our forces are mirroring the Americans' moves," Yichen replied. "When they inch towards us, we do the same." He pointed out to the military shipyard. "Just out there, we have YJ-12B and YJ-62 anti-ship cruise missiles. They are backed by even longer-range missiles on the mainland. You've all seen them. The YJ-12B has a range of about five hundred kilometers. They're carried by almost comical vehicles that look like toy trucks that were scaled up to size. The missiles look pretty, but don't let that fool you. They are deadly."

"Damn right," Lao murmured. "But the YJ-62 missiles *do* look like the war machines that they are. I hope we use them."

"Be careful what you wish for, commander," Yichen said sternly. "It would be better to defeat the Americans without striking a single blow. Don't forget, here on our man-made islands, we have worked hard to develop radar and signals intelligence capabilities. If anything moves on or above the South China Sea, we know about it. And the Americans know that we know. *That* is tactical advantage, even if it isn't directly a lethal weapon. Not every tool at your disposal needs to be a killing machine. Learn that lesson, commanders."

"General," another commander said in a serious voice, "what about brinkmanship via weapons testing?"

"Your head is in the right place, Yang. We've employed this strategy in the past, and it would be straightforward to do it now. Far easier than hampering the Americans' movement through legal methods, and more preferable than outright violence. As you know, we already test our weaponry in order to fend off potential threats. A couple of years ago, we tested a medium-range ballistic missile twice in the South China Sea. And the testing has other benefits—it obstructs other nations' efforts to resupply their outposts in the area."

"Isn't it expensive, though?" Yang asked.

"It's far from free, I concede that much. So, while it might be our best option from a strategic perspective, China's financials might say otherwise. Regardless, we already know that missile testing is an effective strategy. The last time we did this, American journalists told the world that we were threatening them."

"General," Zimo began quietly, "is it wrong that I'm frightened?"

"Young man, no emotion unto itself is wrong. What matters is what you do with it. But if I may mitigate your fears: we have seventy-two fighter jet hangars across our three air bases in the Spratley Islands. We have another sixteen on Woody Island. If it comes to violence, we can deploy combat aircraft very quickly. And we have point defenses, so that if the Americans launch missiles at us, few, if any, would land."

"So what do we do now, General?"

"Stay alert, and pray that this is not the calm before the storm."

United States Air Antonio Bautista Base, Palawan Islands, Philippines

"The Enhanced Defense Cooperation Agreement is proving its worth earlier than expected," Admiral Fuerman said to his peer, Admiral Greer.

The pair was walking around the grassy base, stretching their legs after hours of sedentary meetings. Although neither admiral would admit it, a slow walk against the island's serene, rural backdrop made for a very therapeutic escape from the stresses of their duties.

"Hear, hear," Greer replied. "I remember the Filipino secretary of foreign affairs saying that they wanted to maintain a military alliance with us, following those drawn-out negotiations between our nations. The Chinese won't be happy about our stroke of good fortune."

"We got lucky," Fuerman said. "The Filipinos weren't too happy with China's intrusions into their own waters. Enemy of my enemy, I suppose."

"And I remember that when Manila and Washington made the deal, a State Department spokesman told the media that the Philippines allowed us to have this base more to strengthen our alliance with the Philippines than to keep the Chinese in check. Well, he might've spoken too soon."

Fuerman laughed, but then his jaw tightened. "I saw the look on your face when we were debriefed about potential red lines. Don't worry. I don't think the Chinese can defend the sea territory that they claim. Nor will it stop us from conducting naval operations there."

"Maybe," Greer said doubtingly. "But if they do either …"

Fuerman shook his head. "Remember what else we learned in the debriefing: our military has improved its strategies over the last few years with respect to dealing with the Chinese. The marine corps commandant has come up with some brilliant ideas."

"You sound certain."

"I did more research after the short debriefing. One potential strategy that the commandant has worked out is for us is to enter the waters near China's artificial islands. Then we can send drones, cyber attacks, special forces, and cruise missiles specifically designed to target ships at the Chinese fleet. It's a new age of war."

"Maybe that's why leadership has been so adamant that we press forward, closer and closer to China's bases," Greer said.

"I thought the same thing after my research. The Chinese might talk a big game about how they are the new players on the block, but no one holds a candle to America's military might."

Upon reaching the edge of the base, the pair of admirals turned around to return to their quarters.

"I admit," Greer said, "I felt my spine straighten when we were told about the new tactics."

"Oh, yeah. It's aggressive, but it's just what we need—adding more patrols to the waters around China and her territories. Hopefully it'll send the right message."

Greer waved at some military personnel as they crossed paths before continuing. "I wonder about the Pentagon's efforts to loop our allies into this patrolling endeavor. Don't they want to bring England and France into the South China Sea?"

"Yeah, but why would that be a problem?" Fuerman asked.

"Well, it doesn't *have* to be, but entangling alliances doesn't always end well."

"I'm not sure how useful history is in informing our next choice," Fuerman said. "Every situation is different. You know, I once thought that governments were at their most dangerous when they were being threatened and fighting near home. But then I learned about some exceptions, and I realized that maybe we can't just live by a fixed rule in political decision-making. Life is complicated."

"I guess," Greer said hesitantly. "I read about NATO's plans for the South China Sea. They want to bring even more military forces into the region: Australia, Japan, India, Vietnam, and others. Seems like this would only *add* to the escalating tensions, though."

"Or ... an armed sea is a peaceful sea," Fuerman retorted.

"You're so optimistic, Fuerman."

"I'm just open to all of the ways this could play out. I'm pretty sure—though I'm not positive—that we have the advantage when it comes to brute force. The Chinese can't possibly know about what our air force is up to. We have bombers on other Pacific bases, mostly remote islands. It gives them more wartime flexibility than they've had before. The Chinese won't be expecting such a nimble foe."

The admirals had reached their quarters, which was an almost decadent motel. It stood in stark contrast to both the greenery around them and the robust military vehicles only a quarter-mile away.

The men shared a look with each other, and each knew what the other was thinking.

They did not want to go back inside, where work was waiting for them. They knew that this conversation might be their last moment of reprieve for a long time.

"Apparently, the Chinese aren't backing down," Greer said quietly. "We were told that they'd do that by now."

"They will, eventually," Fuerman responded confidently. "The USS *Ronald Reagan* only recently entered the fray. It sits on the high seas alongside the USS Shiloh and the USS *Halsey*, each carrying our best missile technology. And that's just one example off the top of my head. Our presence in the South China Sea has only been ramping up in recent years. China can't keep up."

Greer released a loud yawn. "Fine, fine. It's been two days since I slept. Things are only getting more tense around here. Think we should get some shut-eye while we can?"

Fuerman smiled lightly at his friend. "In a minute. Let's soak in the sunlight for a little longer."

The pair of admirals stood together in silence, staring out at the calm waters of the South China Sea. They stood with disciplined stoicism, but both were more worried than their body language would admit.

They were well aware that the U.S. Navy was ordered to cross the red line that China drew on the South China Sea and that China was not to claim even more sea territory than was allowed by the International Law of the Seas.

Each man knew that the chances of war were rising with each day.

TWENTY-TWO
★★★
CHAPTER

A delicate knock on the door broke the uneasy silence between Bill and Yao.

"Who is it?" Yao shouted.

"Oh, it's Maggie, one of Secretary Bryers's staff members."

Bill gave Yao a nod and said, "Please, give me a moment. I'll be right back."

The secretary left the breakfast meeting and returned to the hallway, where a tall, muscular woman stood. Bill had known Maggie for six years, ever since she'd graduated college. He had been something of a mentor to her as she learned to navigate the world of Washington, D.C.

"Hey, Maggie," Bill said quietly, so that Yao couldn't hear them. "You seem a little flustered. What's going on?"

"I was told to update you immediately on the South China Sea. It's … it's not good, sir."

Bill crossed his arms. "Please, go on."

"Both militaries are slowly headed towards each other, with neither backing down."

Bill muttered a curse under his breath. "Were you told any predictions about how long until there's a first strike?"

Maggie shook her head. "I wasn't. I'm sorry."

"Please find out and tell me. Also, I can see on your face that there's more. Please, be forward."

"We received intel that Russia is ready to back the Chinese as soon as they need them."

Bill thought of America's own allies that would do the same for them—such as Japan, South Korea, Australia, the United Kingdom, and perhaps India—but he did not say anything. "Russia has a secret alliance with China in the international conflict with the United States. I should've seen that coming. Dammit. Okay, Maggie. Thank you. And if you see any of our other staff or diplomats, please just tell them to relax and stay calm. Above all else, warn them not to get into verbal sparring matches with the Chinese while we're stuck here."

"You got it, Secretary," Maggie said quietly.

Bill narrowed his eyes. "What is everyone else up to?" he asked suspiciously.

"Well … some of our staff *has* been mingling with the Chinese. Um, some grabbed food together, and some are … at the bar."

Bill rubbed his tired eyes. "I've never been a micromanager. I guess fingers crossed that no one comes to blows."

"Actually, some of them seem to be having fun."

"Really? Well, that's a start, I suppose. Anyway, let me get back to it. Thank you, Maggie."

With a grateful nod, Bill quickly returned to the room in which he'd begun private discussions with Yao. By now, the food on the long table was no longer steaming.

As Bill returned to his seat, Yao asked, "Is everything alright?"

Bill pursed his lips. "Not really. But the good news first—it seems that our people are getting along quite well during this unforeseen break."

"What?"

"Yeah, I thought the same thing. I guess in the absence of politics, it's easy for people to get along."

"And yet," Yao said somberly, "it is in diplomacy when getting along matters most."

"I couldn't agree more."

"So. What's the bad news?"

Bill released a heavy breath. "Our countries are on the brink of war. Each side is heading towards the other with no signs of stopping. But it's worse than that. If violence breaks out, your allies and mine will also join the fighting. It could be … God, I can't even say it."

Yao took a sip of his tea. "A world war, I know. I must admit: I fear that we are entering a situation similar to that of World War I."

Bill blinked. "I was just thinking the same thing."

Yao smiled, but it did not reach his eyes. "I know the geopolitical history of Europe quite well. In today's global age, no region's history is entirely disconnected from any other's."

"So you know how World War I got so bloody, then?"

"Yes, Secretary. In 1914, a Serbian patriot shot and killed Archduke Franz Ferdinand, the heir to the Austro-Hungarian Empire. He was killed in order to liberate Bosnia from the boot of the empire, but the unintended consequences of a single act of rebellion brought hell to the continent."

"The archduke would've inherited one of the world's most powerful positions at the time, so the assassination itself was monumental," Bill said. "But that's actually not the part of the story I was thinking of. Leading up to the war, in the late 1800s and early 1900s, Europe's major powers had been building more and more powerful navies and armies. It was a kind of arms race. Countries had secret, mutual defense treaties with each other."

"Ah!" Yao said and clasped his hands. "Much like you currently have with Taiwan! In addition to your publicly announced treaties with Japan and South Korea."

Bill nearly let his frustration get the best of him, but he stopped himself and instead said, "Indeed—as you have alliances with Russia and North Korea. Russia used to be at odds with your country, but now it props up your maritime activities in the open seas. Don't you see that they only do so to stick a thumb in *our* eyes? They are using you."

Yao very slightly bowed his head, and Bill could not tell if the foreign minister was conveying acknowledgement or … respect. "That may be the case, but it is good not to be alone against the West. So many of you send ships across the South China Sea, and we both know it is often only to keep watch on our doings. So yes, we accept Russia's help. I will not apologize for our alliance. Our military makes full use of Russia's technology and wealth of knowledge. They even sold us over twenty combat aircrafts and several S-400 missile systems recently. America is not the only country that is allowed to make uneasy alliances. I understand the precedent that World War I set, but the West leaves us with no choice."

"Anyway," Bill continued, eager to not let this conversation devolve into an argument, "don't you remember the rest of the story of World War I? Austria-Hungary made ruthless demands of Serbia following the assassination. Serbia was told to let Austria-Hungary investigate the assassination, shut down any anti-Austrian media channels within its borders, and destroy all terrorist cells in Serbia. Austria-Hungary's dual monarchy wanted Serbia to accept this ultimatum within forty-eight hours."

"Ah, yes," Yao said as he briefly closed his eyes, tacitly accepting Bill's effort to keep the conversation focused on history. "And then Serbia ran to Russia for help. Its council of ministers felt that the empire was exploiting the assassination as a way to launch a war that it had already wanted to fight. Austria-Hungary did not expect Russia to put its military power behind Serbia, which was a great blunder."

"I agree," Bill said. "Russia mobilized its forces, and then Serbia did the same. The country's prime minister, Nicola Pasic, told Austria-Hungary that he'd accept every aspect of the ultimatum … except one." Bill grinned at Yao as the foreign minister nodded knowingly. "You do know your European history, don't you?"

Yao chuckled. "I'm a man of my word, Secretary. The Serbians would not allow Austria-Hungary to take part in its internal investigation into the assassination. Amazing to think about how different history would have been, had the Serbians just accepted that one final demand. The ambassador of the empire, Baron Giesl von Gieslingen, was not happy with Serbia's refusal to cooperate. Three days later, Austria-Hungary declared that the empire was officially at war with Serbia, and so World War I began."

"Austria-Hungary saw the refusal to accept its terms as an excuse to invade Serbia. They hoped to defeat them quickly, so that Russia wouldn't have time to come help Serbia. But then Germany, a close ally of Austria-Hungary, declared war on Russia."

"Soon after that," Yao added, "France invaded Alsace, and British troops entered France. Then Austria-Hungary invaded Russia. As if

Europe wasn't enough of a mess by this point, Germany invaded Belgium, since Belgium was a French ally. And Britain declared war on Germany—since Britain was a strong ally of France! Honestly, I don't quite remember the exact order of events. Forgive me for any errors, Secretary."

Bill was enjoying this game of historical back-and-forth, and he sensed that Yao was, too. "Your knowledge is impressive enough as it stands. Twenty million people were killed in that war, and twenty million more were wounded. Half of the injured were mere civilians. The lesson is clear."

"Don't assassinate any Chinese official if you're not ready for blowback," Yao said with a wink. "Especially me."

Much to his own surprise, Bill laughed at Yao's rare joke. "Well, sure. But also: entangling alliances don't always keep you safe. An alliance between Britain, France, and Russia was signed in 1907. One would think that such a pact would have kept them safe, and yet look what happened less than a decade later. Entangling alliances are a double-edged sword."

"Your concern that we are on the brink of another World War I situation is well-placed," Yao asserted flatly.

"No, I think we're headed towards something much, much worse."

The two leaders sat in worried silence.

"I remember something else about that war," Yao said after several seconds. "Germany felt that they were surrounded by enemies. Meanwhile, France and Russia were keen to put Germany down while they still could, before the country grew even more powerful." He raised an eyebrow at Bill. "Our intelligence tells us that America thinks that she should fight *us* now, before we become too strong to take on."

Bill looked away, uncomfortable at the accusation.

"I understand your concern," Yao continued. "If I was in your position, I'd feel the same way."

Bill's eyes returned to Yao. "Frankly, it doesn't matter what America thinks about your trajectory as a global superpower. We have more pressing concerns."

"No?" Yao asked skeptically. "Is it not in the back of America's mind that the current tension in the South China Sea is exactly the pretense it needs to attack?"

"I don't speak for anyone but myself," Bill said. "I don't want war. Does China concern me? Honestly? Yes, it does. But the world can't afford another World War I debacle, and this mess is no archduke assassination. Wars often begin following each side misunderstanding and miscalculating the other. War War I is the prime example."

There was another stretch of silence, this one less friendly than the last.

Finally, Yao said, "You have changed."

Bill frowned. "What?"

"You are far humbler than you once were. Your spirit is more ... humanitarian, or so it seems."

"Um ... thank you, I think. But I've always wanted peace on earth."

"I would not have known that from the last time we were together. You were arrogant. Narcissistic. Cared more about fame than solving problems."

"What the hell? Excuse my language, Foreign Minister, but I've cared about my work for decades. Is this why you voted against my nomination for secretary-general of the United Nations? Because you didn't like my personality?"

"No, actually," Yao said calmly. "It's true that I did not think highly of you at the time. But my vote against you was not my decision."

"Wait, what?"

Yao shook his head. "I was ordered to vote against you. I didn't ask why."

Bill thought back to that time in his life. "I had a record of settling disputes between political factions across the globe. I don't understand ..."

Yao shrugged, but his expression was sincere. "I can't help you. I'm sorry."

Bill shook his head. "Let's agree to leave it in the past." He leaned forward and extended his hand. "You say that you think I changed for the better. Let me prove it. Work with me, Foreign Minister. And we can prevent war from swallowing the world."

Yao stared at Bill's hand.

And he waved it away.

"I'm sorry, Secretary. I'm still suspicious of you and the rest of your country. But let me extend an intermittent peace talking. I'd like to continue speaking with you later in the day. And maybe, if you can persuade me of you and your people's noble intentions, I will shake your hand."

Bill sat back, frustrated. *We were so close. But it's not over yet.*

"That's a deal," Bill said. "Let's talk to our staff and our political leaders first. Then I say we meet for lunch."

"Let's do it."

TWENTY-THREE
★★★
CHAPTER

Um, don't mind my bed. I was going to make it later, I promise."

Guo smiled at Josh and took a seat in his room's chair, while Josh walked nervously over to the little refrigerator.

"Okay … you said you wanted beer, right? Not sure how good it'll be, but here you go."

Josh tossed a beer can to Guo, who caught it with one hand.

"Thanks," she said. "I just wanted to get away from everyone for a bit. I'm a bit of an introvert. I appreciate you inviting me over."

Josh opened his beer and took a swig. "My pleasure. You looked like you could use some away time. I know the feeling."

"Before you came over to me, I saw you with some of the delegates," Guo said. "Your body was present, but your mind was distant. Is everything okay?"

Josh nearly panicked, but he managed to maintain his poker face. *Stay cool. She doesn't know anything.* "Yeah, I'm fine, thanks. It's just … don't you think it's weird to see everyone getting along all of a sudden? Like it's one damn big party. But it's not, you know? There's so much at stake, and we're acting like our countries aren't on the verge of war."

Guo flipped her long hair back, and for the first time, Josh noticed how beautiful she was, even without any makeup. "The crisis in the South China Sea is out of our hands at the moment. And our peoples are getting along. Isn't that a good thing?"

Josh looked away from Guo for a moment. "Um, right, yeah. I'm sorry, I'm just thrown off by the fact that we're stuck here. I'm on edge."

"Just relax, Josh. We're not working right now. There's nothing to worry about. And for the record, Bill and Yao are speaking with each other right now. Or at least, they were as of an hour ago. So maybe everything will work out for the best."

Josh thought of the black dot that he was hiding behind his palm. He took a deep swig of his drink. "You're right. I'm sorry. So … where are you from?"

Guo laughed, and to Josh's surprise, the sound relaxed him. "Really? That's the most clichéd opener to a conversation of all time. But fine, I'll take it. I grew up in a village called Niujie. The scenery was gorgeous, but I always itched to leave the rural life and live in the city. My family ran a simple farm, but I did well in school. I excelled at languages especially. I am fluent in seven of them. I was placed on a fast track to a diplomatic career. One thing led to the next, and here I am. How about you?"

Josh walked over to his window and leaned against it, so that he was even more distant from Guo. "My dad was in the armed forces, so I didn't grow up in any one place. I spent some time in Asia as a kid, actually, and the American military base in Japan was terrific. I've lived on every continent but Antarctica and South America. When I was seventeen, we settled down in a working-class neighborhood in Ohio."

"Why did you settle down? Also, I don't bite, Josh. You can come closer."

Josh frowned but took a few tentative steps closer until he sat on the floor next to Guo, who remained in her chair. "My dad was kicked out of the military. I hated him for it at the time. Hell, maybe I still do. We come from a long line of public servants. I have ancestors who fought in the Civil War, the War of 1812, and even the Revolutionary War. Not sure if you know what those are, but they're pivotal moments in our history."

Guo laughed again, and Josh's heart beat faster. "I'm a student of American history, so yes I'm familiar. I'm sorry to hear about your father, though."

"Yeah," Josh muttered. "Ever since he was shunned, I've had a chip on my shoulder. To this day, I want to make things right. I want every holiday with the family to not be awkward. I want to be able to tell my future kids that they can be proud of their lineage. It's like there's a black cloud over my head, and everyone can see it."

"I don't see it," Guo said delicately. "I won't ask what your father did. And I know what it's like for familial shame to carry on to the next generation. My grandfather killed someone, back when he was young. I still don't really know for sure what the circumstances were. My parents don't talk about it. But as a kid back home in Niujie, I'd hear the other villagers whisper. I think it was over a land dispute with a neighbor, but I've never bothered to find out the truth."

Josh looked up at Guo, whose smile looked so inviting. "Is that the real reason you left?"

"It certainly didn't help to keep me there. But no, I think I've always craved adventure. The desire to roam the earth, to learn about what *all* of humanity has to offer. It's always been who I am. And here you are, a man who's already lived all over the world!"

Josh swallowed, suddenly overwhelmed with conflicting emotions. "Yeah, I think you would've appreciated it more than I ever did. All I wanted as a kid was to achieve something. Anything, really. I never did well in school, and moving around so much made it hard to make friends."

"You seem pretty successful now," Guo said sincerely.

"Thanks," Josh said dismissively. "But time will tell. And I … I admire your spirit, Guo. You've been able to escape from the shadow that follows your family. I haven't. Not yet anyway. But I …" His throat tightened up, and he forced some beer down in order to hide the fact that he was becoming so emotional. "I've been asked to do things, Guo. Things that could redeem my family name."

"Josh? You're confusing me."

He pursed his lips and shook his head. "Never mind. I'm so sorry. I know you just wanted to relax, and here I am, acting like a weak prey animal."

"Don't be sorry. I like your honesty. In fact, I really like it. Do you know why I have a hard time with large crowds?"

"Of course I don't," Josh said, trying hard to smile. "I barely know you."

Guo rose from her chair and sat cross-legged next to Josh. "The larger a group gets, the less authentic each individual becomes. To be honest, I don't even enjoy all of the formalities we have to express during our diplomatic meetings. But I grit my teeth and bear it because I love contributing to China's success."

There was a long pause before Josh responded. "You know," he finally said, "you come off very differently in private than you do when you're around everyone else. But I guess that makes sense, given what you've told me."

Guo laughed. "Are you shy?"

"No. Why?"

"Because for the assistant secretary of state, you seem nervous to be alone with a woman. You're a powerful man, no?"

Josh recalled Bannister's orders, and he gripped his hand tightly over the black dot. "Hey, don't tell me you're familiar with America's political organizational charts, too?" he asked teasingly, trying to bring some levity to the conversation.

"I studied up on your Department of State the last few days. I figured it would be useful. Let's see if I can remember ... you are responsible for assisting the secretary on diplomatic negotiations."

Josh smiled. "Something like that, yeah. I'm the youngest one in history. Did you know that?"

Guo put her beer can down and slid an inch closer to Josh. "No, I didn't. Are you trying to impress me?"

"What? No, I, um—"

Guo leaned forward and kissed Josh.

His heart was racing by now. He kissed her back, slowly at first, then more passionately. He wrapped his right arm around her back, never forgetting the black dot in his left hand. Josh gently leaned her back towards the floor and, as he did, slid his open left hand across her backside. He had the opportunity to place the black dot onto Guo's shirt, but he chose not to go through with it.

"Wait," Josh said after he pulled his lips from Guo's. "I'm ... I'm not sure this is right. Too fast."

"Okay," she whispered. "I'm sorry if I made you uncomfortable."

Josh rose to his feet and paced back and forth a few times. "No, of course not. You're amazing. I just …"

Guo stood up and stared at Josh with warm eyes. "You're still stressed. I see that."

"Under normal circumstances, I'd want nothing more than to keep kissing you. I just have some things I have to do. I wish I could say more, but I have difficult choices to make, and they won't get out of my head."

Guo rushed over to Josh, took his hands, and petted them slowly. "Do you have a chance to redeem your family name?"

"Yeah. I think I do."

"Then do it, and don't look back. I'm headed to my room. Let's catch up later, okay? You can tell me how it went. Whatever it is—I'll never ask."

Josh's heart sank with the heavy weight of guilt and shame of what he almost did. "I'd like that. Maybe we can get drinks tonight. I mean, more drinks."

Guo laughed. "I'd like that. Goodbye, Josh."

As soon as Guo left, Josh muttered a defeated curse to himself.

What did I just do? I disobeyed Bannister. I like Guo. Unlike Bannister, she respects me. Maybe admires me, even. Is my family name that important to me? Am I such a weak man?

Josh's features tightened as adamant focus replaced his confused feelings of attraction and guilt.

I've had enough of your bullying, Bannister.

"Who's there?" Bannister's gruff voice called.

"It's me," Josh said from the other side of the door.

Bannister opened the door and gave Josh a contemptuous glance before letting him in.

"Why are you in a bathrobe at this hour?" Josh asked.

"Excuse me?"

Josh sneered. "I didn't do what you asked. I didn't put the recording device on Guo. Happy?"

"Watch your tone, boy. What's wrong with you?"

Josh shook his head. "Nothing, alright? We done here? Bannister, you keep your end of the bargain, and we don't have to cross paths again."

"I'm a man of my word, Joshy. When diplomacy fails and we defeat China in the war to come, you'll receive the glory you deserve. And you'll bring the honor back to your family that your father spoiled so many years ago. But no, we're not finished yet. Did you think I'd forget? You think I'm stupid?"

Josh huffed but accepted his fate. "What's next, then? I won't betray Guo's innocence."

"I already told you. Use the Dictaphone to record Bill talking smack about the Chinese. That too tall an order for you?"

"No. I'll get it done. Aren't Bill and Yao talking now, though?"

Bannister frowned and put his hands to his hips. "You're smart, you'll figure it out. What happened with Guo that has you so screwed up?"

"Nothing."

Bannister grinned mockingly. "I see. Well, you can die knowing that your handsome face was not useful at least once in your life. But you can still help us achieve our mission."

"Oh yeah? Enlighten me."

"Use your head, boy. The delegations had already failed without your intervention, and we were set to return home. Now that Yao and Bill have a second chance to patch things up, *you* have a second chance to save the day."

"Save the day," Josh spat. "You're so confident that you're in the right. What if—"

Bannister rushed towards Josh and pointed a finger in his face. "Don't you dare question me, boy! Have you forgotten what I can do to your family? You have no idea the depths I can drag you down to. I know the truth about what your father did. Don't cross me. Now, get out and get it done."

Josh slammed Bannister's door on the way out.

TWENTY-FOUR
★★★
CHAPTER

B ill chose to remain standing, even while the rest of the diplomats took their seats around the conference table. The secretary of state quietly watched as his team chatted amongst themselves, full of energy.

It's odd to see them dressed so casually, he thought. *Ah, but I guess they got dressed thinking they were headed home this morning. Funny how their casual dress affects their behavior.*

Bill clapped his hands, and the room fell silent. "Hi, everyone. Thank you for joining me. We need to work quickly. I am told that you all had productive, informal meetings with your counterparts. Well done!

"As some of you know, I spoke with Yao Sheng this morning. I have to admit, it did not go badly. I wouldn't get too excited, but I think there is hope for diplomacy, after all. The bad news is that if we don't act quickly, we could have a war on our hands. But before we engage in further diplomacy, I thought we'd have a planning session together."

Bill took a breath and let his update sink in before continuing. "Now, during breakfast, my staff told me that I needed to put on the news. I figured we would watch it together, while we work on a peace proposal to bring to Yao." He pointed at Sara, who sat at the other end of the table and held a remote control in her hand. "Please, go ahead."

Sara turned on the television that hung against the wall next to her seat. After flipping through a few Chinese channels, Bill finally said, "Stop there. Let's see what's happening on the BBC."

"…dangerous situation in the South China Sea," a woman said in an English accent. She was sitting in a studio with another well-dressed anchor.

Bill noticed that both anchors wore tight, grim expressions. They were professionally composed, but Bill could read the tension on their faces.

"It's hard to describe it as anything else," the male anchor said. "As you saw in the last clip we played, the American and Chinese navies are heading towards each other at a steady pace. One of them could accelerate at a moment's notice and fire upon the other, and we'd have war on our hands in no time."

"I want to add to that, Paul," the other anchor said. "Reports indicate that countries all over Asia are mobilizing their militaries."

"Hilary, let's give the viewers an update on South Korea."

In between the news anchors, images of military vehicles and soldiers appeared on the screen.

"These are recent photographs taken in South Korea," Paul continued. "Only in the last hour, we have confirmed that the American military forces already in the area have joined the South Koreans in their anticipation of a North Korean attack."

"The allies are on high alert," Hilary said. "Apparently, North Korea began to mobilize their armed forces less than twelve hours ago. The dangerous, one-hundred-and-sixty-mile demilitarized zone that separates two countries that are officially still at war, North and South Korea, may be on the brink of chaos."

"An anonymous source told us that South Korean officials are concerned that North Korea will exploit the situation in the South China Sea," Paul said. "With America preoccupied with China, the North Koreans think that they can make their move against their southern neighbors."

"Our prayers are with all of the peaceful citizens of South Korea," Hilary said somberly. "Paul, what else is happening around the world?"

The image between the news anchors faded away. A few seconds later, a new picture replaced it, this one of a Japanese flag rippling in the wind.

"Hilary, in just the last few hours, we've received word that Japan is pledging troops to help protect both South Korea and Taiwan. The Japanese navy is on high alert as well."

"This is quite unsettling, Paul. Why don't we share with viewers the latest on the American protests?"

The image of the Japanese flag was replaced with video footage of numerous protests and riots. Bill swallowed as he took in the violent visuals.

Chicago, Los Angeles, Philadelphia, Boston, Dallas, New York ... Washington, D.C., he thought to himself as video from each city played on the television.

"In every city, the protests appear to be two-sided," Hilary said. "As you can see from this footage from the United States capital, one side carries signs with anti-war messages, while the other is extremely anti-China. We received footage featuring the two sides clashing in streets across America's urban centers, but much of it is too violent to share."

"Two people have died during the riots so far," Paul added. "The National Guard has been mobilized across the country in order to control the violence."

"This is getting out of control," Bill murmured to himself. "I'm sorry, all," he said, loudly enough for everyone to hear. "I know I said that we'd have another round of diplomacy later, but I was wrong: we clearly don't have time. I have to go."

Bill left the conference room and immediately bumped into Marc, the CIA mission chief for China. He was holding an electronic tablet.

"Secretary," Marc said seriously, and then gestured for Bill to look at his tablet. "Just the man I was looking for. You need to see this. It's an intelligence report, and it's for your eyes only."

"Ah, thank you," Bill said, and then he took the tablet into his hands and read the document on it.

When he finished, he handed the tablet back to Marc, who quickly deleted the document.

"Bill, I trust that you know what you need to do."

Bill did his best to keep his composure, despite his rising anxiety. "Yes, yes. Thank you, Marc."

With a polite nod, Marc walked away.

Bill returned to his conference room and announced, "All, please draft me some compromise points for negotiations with Yao. I'm going to find him in the meantime. Thank you."

Bill once again left the room and walked around until he found the nearest lodge staff member.

"Hi, excuse me. Do you know where Foreign Minister Yao and his diplomats are right now?"

The Chinese diplomats sat in their own conference room, all eyes glued to the television.

Yao was hardly paying attention to the news anchors, since he was receiving a briefing by Chinese intelligence on the situation in hushed whispers.

"Russia is mobilizing their navy and has sent submarines to the South China Sea," the Chinese anchorwoman said. "They have also sent war supplies to Chinese forces in the area. Thus far, they have shown themselves to be loyal allies in the fight against the Western imperialists."

"Indeed," the anchorman said to his cohost. "There is fervent activity all across the continent. The Taiwanese government has put the island on full alert, in preparation for a possible invasion by our own government."

"I find that quite interesting, Chao. They are clearly thinking several steps ahead, since we are surely too preoccupied in the South China Sea to invade Taiwan. Perhaps they are reading too many hyperbolic media reports. Taiwan's defense minister said that we would be capable of launching a brutal invasion of the island in just a few years."

"As usual, Taiwan is exposing its own paranoia. Vietnam, too, is anticipating an invasion. Perhaps memories of the Sino-Vietnamese War are still fresh in their minds. Even their friends from the Soviet Union were unable to save them back then. I remember how easily we were able to capture their cities."

"Yes, perhaps Vietnam will think more carefully this time about who it wishes to align itself with. Meanwhile, anti-American protests have broken out in Beijing."

Images of Chinese protestors marching along Beijing's streets were shown. They carried placards with signs such as "No more imperialists" and "Down with the U.S.A."

"What do you think, Ju?" Chao asked.

"I think that … the Chinese people are very smart. They know what the right side of history is. Times like these are when I am most grateful that we are such a unified people."

"While *our* protestors are wise and peaceful," Chao responded, "the American protestors are the opposite. They disagree with each other about what their government should do, and they have come to blows!"

"To be expected," Ju said. "The Americans are always at each other's throats. It is perhaps the greatest weakness of democracy. Let's show footage from the recent riot in Washington, D.C."

By now, the Chinese intelligence agents had stopped talking, and Yao's attention had drifted to the television. His jaw dropped as he took in the scene. Policemen were everywhere, trash littered the streets, and rioters were shattering storefronts. As the camera zoomed out, a smoke bomb went off, and the footage ended as screams erupted—screams that shook Yao to his bones.

"We also discovered an interview between an American journalist and one of the rioters," Ju said. "Let's show that to the viewers."

The screen suddenly showed a young man in a black sweatshirt, standing at the foot of an alleyway. His brown hair was disheveled, and dirt and blood marked his thin neck.

A female interviewer stood next to him, holding a microphone up to him. "Could you please tell me what you've been doing here today?"

"We're here to stop America from imposing its will on other countries!" he said aggressively. "The U.S. empire has been terrorizing peoples across the world for a long time. We refuse to let our tax dollars go to another mass murder campaign. Vietnam, Iraq, Afghanistan … we've done enough damage!"

"Do you support the Chinese government?" the interviewer asked.

"I don't care about it," the kid said. "The point is, it's not our business. Do you know how many foreign wars we fight? It's crazy, and it always leads to more oppression in the end, not more democracy."

"And were you part of the riots earlier today?"

"Hell yeah, I was. The pigs tried to stop us from expressing our First Amendment rights. That doesn't fly with us."

"Are you aware that at least two people are dead?"

The kid rolled his eyes. "How many people has the United States government killed, and no one ever asks them about it? We're speaking truth to power. Of course it's risky, and I hate that people have died. But what else are we going to do? Let the war machine start World War III, just so that the military-industrial establishment makes a profit? I don't think so."

The footage ended and was quickly replaced by another interviewer standing next to a middle-aged man in a hat and plaid jacket. He was holding up a placard that said, "CHINA'S TIME IS NOT NOW."

"Hello, sir," the interviewer said. "What, exactly, are you protesting?"

"I'm here with a group of veterans," he said calmly but confidently. "China is becoming far too powerful on the world stage. You know, many of us thought that it would become a liberal democracy after its economic reforms of the 1970s, but it's clear that didn't happen. As the protectors of the world, we have a duty to prevent China from expanding its territory and bringing communism and dictatorship to more parts of the world."

"Are you prepared to go to war?" the interviewer asked.

"I think when a great evil presents itself, there are no pretty answers. Yes, war is sometimes necessary. I believe that China is a grave enough threat that America should take it on."

"But will you personally fight the Chinese and their allies?"

"Of course I will," the veteran answered. "My grandpa fought the Nazis in World War II. My dad was in Vietnam. The least I can do is follow in their footsteps of public service."

"What do you think of those who say that America should keep to herself?"

The veteran frowned at that. "You know, I see a lot of these anti-war protestors, most of them very young. I get that it sounds good to say that you're for peace, but that doesn't fly when the enemy doesn't give a damn about your precious peace. So I think that the isolationists mean well, but they're too naïve. We need to fight back against China. Hell, if we have to invade the mainland, we should."

"That's enough," Yao said from his seat. "Please, turn it off."

The room was utterly silent as Yao rubbed his forehead.

Finally, Yao said to his team, "I have to act now. There is no more time."

"What about us?" one of the diplomats asked.

"Wait here, please. I'm going to speak with Secretary Bryers once more. I'm sorry, I cannot answer any more questions right now. We have to prevent this war."

Without another word, Yao rose to his feet and left the conference room. To his surprise, he nearly bumped right into Bill, who had been walking briskly towards him.

"Oh, good!" Bill said between quick breaths. "Yao, I just watched the news with my diplomats. We need to—"

Yao put a hand on Bill's shoulder. "I know. We did the same. Let's return to the room in which we had breakfast."

Bill's tense posture noticeably relaxed. "Thank God. I have some ideas, but ..."

Bill paused as the pair began to walk very quickly.

"What is it?" Yao asked.

"I'll tell you when we're completely alone. I received some intel earlier today, after we had breakfast. You'll see ..."

"Alright, Secretary. I'm putting my trust in you."

Bill turned to Yao. "Thank you, Foreign Minister. Let's go stop this war."

TWENTY-FIVE
★★
CHAPTER

Yao and Bill returned to the room in which they had eaten breakfast. Now, though, the table was completely barren.

Bill found that fitting. *This is no time for a meal.*

The leaders sat across from each other and shared eye contact for a long while before Yao broke the silence.

"Like I said," Yao began, "I am putting my trust in you. What's on your mind?"

Bill nervously rubbed his hands together. "Let's talk about China's red line."

Yao furrowed his eyebrows but nodded. "Of course."

Bill eyed the door to the conference room, even though it had been shut since they entered. They kept silent as a woman knocked, entered, and poured them each a cup of tea.

"Listen, Foreign Minister," Bill began. "What I'm about to tell you can never leave this room. I'm about to violate every protocol, every oath that I've sworn, every law in the book." Bill nearly continued, but he choked up and his hands started shaking.

Yao swallowed but waited for Bill to finish his thought.

"Okay." Bill breathed. "China drew a red line in the South China Sea that the United States is not to cross, or else it would be considered a declaration of war. Well, the U.S. Navy plans to cross that line."

Shocked, Yao let out a tiny noise. "What? But … why? When will they do this? They can't!"

"Tomorrow," Bill answered solemnly. "Unless … unless we act now, Foreign Minister. We can stop this. It is easy to start a war but hard to end one. I know my country has been aggressive in the past, and maybe you'll never agree with some of our foreign policy decisions. But we are an honorable nation. If we showed the world that we came to a diplomatic agreement, our military would not strike. We are both students of history. You know as well as I do that most wars begin following a tragic series of miscalculations and misunderstandings. But the fate of this conflict is not written in stone. We can end this series of accidents, subterfuge, and impending attacks."

Yao rubbed his eyes, paused, and then asked, "Secretary, what else do you know?"

"I was told that Russia is going to help China if we attack. We're looking at a multinational conflict here. Russia and China have been in conflict since Mao's time. We know they have become united against the U.S. You don't have to admit it; I know that mutual suspicion has been brewing."

Yao laughed mirthlessly. "Only a few months ago, our president called Russia's president his dearest friend. Of course, I knew that it was only for show. The Russian president lied through his teeth, saying that we were on our way to becoming strategic allies. They really want China to challenge the United States. This would be a win for Russia at little cost to itself."

Yao stroked his chin as he thought about it further. "I think that North Korea would invade South Korea, too. They'd exploit the fact that you will be too preoccupied to protect your ally." Yao placed two determined fists on the table. "Secretary, I appreciate you risking your career by telling me the truth."

Bill blinked away a couple of tears. "I didn't do it for you. I did it for the peoples of the world. But Foreign Minister, I do trust you now. We have the same mission."

"We have to act for the sake of humanity," Yao agreed. "We must stop the senseless slaughter that is on the horizon. I should tell you something, in the spirit of mutual trust."

"What is it?" Bill asked with concern.

"I don't mean to sound aggressive or condescending, but your country is no longer the world's most powerful military. We have recently tested a novel weapon."

Bill frowned. "Okay?"

"It's a nuclear-capable hypersonic missile. It has already traversed the entire globe, carrying a hypersonic glide vehicle through low-orbit space before cruising down towards its target. You might be able to hunt down our ballistic missiles and neutralize them before they reach their target, but unless you know something I don't, our hypersonic missile is too powerful for you to defend against. The glide vehicle is capable of being armed with a nuclear warhead and does not follow the fixed parabolic trajectory of a ballistic missile, making it difficult to outmaneuver. We will be able to strike you wherever and whenever we want."

Bill's jaw dropped, but he quickly regained his composure. *I … I don't know of any American defenses that can contend with such a weapon*, he thought to himself.

"Secretary, the next war between global superpowers will not resemble World War II or the World War I. I know that your country avoided most of the bloodshed in World War II. But please, understand that the next global war will not spare you. You won't just have our hypersonic missiles to worry about, either. In the age of the Internet, our cybersecurity attacks and artificial intelligence can bring the United States to her knees."

I'm concerned that our intelligence agencies have not reported on your new weapon, Bill thought to himself. *I'm in regular contact with them; I would've known. Our intelligence community is composed of nearly twenty organizations, and they are given nearly one hundred billion dollars annually to discover secrets such as this one. Either they have declined in their effectiveness, or else you and your people have become more adept at hiding your projects.*

"It would not be a one-sided victory," Yao said, "but I will say that we have become quite capable in a number of areas. From what I understand, the West underestimates us."

Bill nodded. "In World War I, twenty million people lost their lives. In World War II, it was over fifty million. If we suffer through World War III, we could lose hundreds of millions of people. It's the nuclear age, after all."

There was a heavy pause, during which Bill thought about his family.

Finally, Yao said in a calm voice, "My wife was always my inspiration. She was so loving, so devoted to everything she did. I just want her to be proud of me, Secretary. Wherever her soul is, I don't want her to see me fail our daughter and granddaughter. I don't want her to witness me failing all of my countrymen if this war gets out of control. For her, China, and the world, we need to come to an agreement."

"I hear you," Bill said. "My wife sometimes thinks I don't need her, but the truth is that I crave her approval. She's the strongest person I've ever known. I can't fail her either."

"Well, then," Yao said with a touch of sadness. "We have to work out a compromise. You have extended an olive branch to me by telling me your military's secret. I did the same. I know I can trust you."

Bill nodded. "We need a map of the South China Sea. I'll be right back."

The secretary of state left the room and walked briskly towards the room in which his staff was still meeting.

He thought of his family and how badly he wanted to call them.

But I can't, he thought apologetically. *When this is all over, we'll go on a long family vacation … if I succeed. If I don't, well … stop it, Bill. This is no time for pessimism.*

He reached the room, where his diplomats all eyed him at once.

"Bill," Sara said with concern.

Bill forced the panic in his chest from affecting his demeanor. "Hi again. Please bring me a map of the South China Sea with China's claims marked."

"You're not going to give into their claims, are you?" Josh asked. "I can see it on your face."

Bill glanced at Josh but said nothing.

"Yes, I can get you that, Bill," Sara responded. "I have to get it from our inventory, which will take me a few minutes. Do you mind waiting here for a bit?"

Yes, I do, Bill thought.

"No problem," he said calmly.

As Sara walked out of the room, the secretary of state eyed the phone sitting idly on his desk.

I have a minute, he thought, and practically dove for the phone.

Bill dialed a number and tapped his foot anxiously as the phone rang. He did not care that everyone could hear him.

"Hello?" a young woman's voice said.

"Samantha," Bill uttered softly. "H-how are you? It's your old man."

Samantha chuckled. "I know who it is, Dad. I'm very sad, but I'm holding up. We all are. I can't believe he's gone. We are delaying the funeral until you return. I know how close you were."

"I lost a son ..." Bill's eyes watered, and he struggled to finish his sentence. "Thanks, sweetheart. Listen, I know what you've been going through, ever since ..."

"It's alright, Dad. Jack died on the sea, where he felt most at home. Gabrielle has been doing a great job of comforting the kids. Now I just want you to come home safely."

"She's a great aunt." Bill thought back to the treason he'd committed only a few minutes earlier. "You're so strong, Samantha. Just like your mother."

"Dad ... is everything okay?"

Bill wiped his face, took a deep breath, and said in a shaky voice, "Yes, everything's fine. I just wanted to tell you that I love you."

"I love you too, Dad," Samantha said sincerely.

Bill hung up and went to dial another number, but he was interrupted by Sara and another intelligence officer, who entered the room and conspicuously placed the map down in front of Bill

Bill delicately grabbed it by one of its corners. "Thank you," he said to Sara and the other officer, and quickly walked back towards the room in which Yao was waiting.

I can't believe he committed treason, Yao thought as he sat in solitude. *Either he is a truly reckless man or else his commitment to world peace is greater than his desire for self-preservation. And he trusts me.*

He doesn't know that, when I told him about our novel weaponry, I also committed treason. I said it so willingly! Is Bill no longer my adversary? I really like him, and I admire his courage.

Yao imagined his father advising him about the situation. *He would have told me to never trust a Westerner except Marx*, Yao mused. *But my father was mistaken, I think. We don't have to live with the Americans to break bread with them. We don't have to absorb their culture to learn from them. And we certainly don't have to squabble over territory in order to maintain peace with them.*

Perhaps my optimism is merely temporary. If Bill returns and displays American arrogance at the start of our negotiations, I will know that my newfound respect for him has been misplaced. But I should not countenance such a possibility. The stakes are too great. We need an agreement that saves face for both China and the U.S.

Yao closed his eyes and leaned his head back, enjoying this brief respite.

A few minutes later, Bill knocked on the door and then reentered the conference room, holding a map of the South China Sea. He placed it on the table, in between the two leaders' chairs.

Bill sat back down and said, "Did I wake you?"

Yao blinked, and it took him a moment to realize that Bill was joking. "Funny man," he said with a grin. Then, in a clearly sarcastic tone, "I was running some equations in my head. I have discovered the perfect compromise to our negotiations. You cannot argue with math."

Bill snorted. "On that, we agree. Unfortunately, this is diplomacy. So. Would you like to speak first?"

Yao leaned back in his chair. *Not arrogant in the slightest. Maybe we can succeed, after all.*

"It would be my honor."

TWENTY-SIX
★★★
CHAPTER

A large flotilla of United States Navy ships floated along the calm waters of the South China Sea. A Chinese fishing boat sat in the middle of the flotilla. The Chinese fishermen's hands shook as they stared wide-eyed at the stoic titans before them. The ships were huge and gray, and weapons of all kinds jutted from their sides.

But the fishermen were confident that they did not intend to fire at them.

The Americans might not know just how powerful we are, one of them thought to himself, *but surely they understand enough that to kill us would mean brutal retaliation.*

Something else that the Americans did not know was that the fishermen were not actually fishermen at all. They were spies for the Chinese government. Unseen devices on the boat were currently broadcasting this showdown to planes on China's nearby artificial island. Those planes, in turn, were feeding the footage to the BBC and Chinese news stations. The news station did not know the spies' true identities, but all of the spies knew that the footage would grab too many eyeballs for the news anchors to refuse it.

One of the fishermen looked down at his shaking hands once more and forced himself not to grin. *They will pay for disrespecting China.*

"You have come too close!" a booming American voice came from one of the ships' speaker systems in perfect Chinese.

"Turn your boat around now, or we will fire!"

The spies steered their vessel *towards* the enemy.

"This is your second warning!" the Americans said, again in Mandarin. "You must distance yourself!"

The spies carried onwards without hesitation.

"Final warning! You have five seconds! Four! Three! Two! One!"

A Chinese drone flew over the scene. It documented a clear picture of the fishing boat, just as it exploded.

London, England

"Oh, my goodness," BBC anchorwoman Hilary said. "Folks, we have horrific footage from the South China Sea. This is a live feed, and we did not expect sudden violence. This is shocking."

"I am in shock as well," Paul responded. "It is unclear at this time if the fishermen were Chinese or of another nationality. It is likely that they were Chinese, given the location. But I don't want to jump to conclusions."

"For sure, Paul. But if they were Chinese, then we may have witnessed the first official civilian casualty in ... a war between China and the United States."

South China Sea

"Mr. President," Admiral Wallace said over the phone. "We are on track to fulfill your demand. Prudence demands that I ask once more: Are you sure you want us to do this?"

"Absolutely," the president said without missing a beat. "Enter the territory that China claims is theirs. Pass the red line. They can't just claim it as their own international waters. Ready our battle stations to the fullest. CIA intelligence tells us that they will not fire upon you." Loudly, he said, "Now go and pass that red line, Admiral."

Wallace clenched his jaw. He was terrified but he had joined the navy precisely for moments like this. "Yes, Mr. President."

"Excellent."

"You're doing the right thing," another voice said through the phone.

Wallace nodded. He knew that the president was currently with his top national security advisor. "Thank you."

Wallace hung up the phone and used his direct line through the secured intercom.

"Captain Singal speaking."

"Captain, it's Admiral Wallace."

There was a heavy pause. "I know you well, Admiral Wallace. The president stands firm in his decision, doesn't he?"

Wallace licked his lips. "That's right. Signal the fleet. We are crossing China's red line."

Spratley Islands, South China Sea

"My goodness," Commodore Liu said as he watched the screen in his headquarters.

The Americans are really doing it, he thought in amazement. *They're crossing a red line. They want war.*

He quickly rose to his feet, picked up the room's phone, and called his superiors at the Ministry of National Defense. After speaking with more than one bureaucrat, he finally came into communication with someone who could help.

"This is Minister Qiang."

"Minister!" Liu exclaimed. "The Americans are broaching one of our red lines. Please, give us your command."

"You must send us confirming evidence of this," Qiang replied calmly. "I take it you can do that in short order."

Liu nodded. "Absolutely."

"Good. Do it now."

Liu darted to his keyboard. He then recorded the live feed on his computer screen and sent the link to China's central control center via a secured and encrypted link.

"Okay," Liu said. "Please let me know when you receive it."

"Yes, one moment ... ah. Received."

Liu could not contain himself. "Please, Minister, tell us what to do!"

"It should be obvious," Qiang said impatiently. "I need our president's approval, but when you receive the confirmed orders from me, destroy all ships that cross the red line. By any means necessary.

But caution is also your friend. Wait to see just how much further they push. I will ask the president what he thinks. Meanwhile, I will give them three hours to leave our territory before we attack."

Summit Lodge, China

Bannister held the phone tightly in his hand as adrenaline began to course through him.

"Mr. President, now is the time," he urged.

"Bannister, we can't just attack them with everything we have, for a number of reasons. This debacle with the fishermen has already turned public opinion against us. Plus, the CIA told me that China will absolutely not attack first."

"Ignore the CIA," Bannister said impatiently. "They're often wrong about China's intentions. Whether China is going to attack us or not, this is a golden opportunity to set back their navy for nearly a decade. We need to take this strategic opportunity. Look, I'm not advising you to drop nuclear bombs on mainland China. The Chinese are bound to attack us once we cross the red line. We should launch a preemptive attack."

"I don't know, Bannister. I can hear the narrative already: 'America attacks China to start World War III.'"

"Damn the headlines," Bannister seethed. "Forget about your short-term reputation, Mr. President. In the long run, righteous statesmen are always recognized for the heroes that they really were. The Chinese are building a navy to match ours. We must defeat them now. In a few years, they will be too powerful to fight. By then, they'll claim any sea territory they want in the South China Sea as their own. All of our allies near China—Japan, South Korea, Taiwan, and the Philippines—are in grave danger. We must stop China's expansion now."

The president sighed into the phone. "You are right about China, Bannister. Curse you. I'm all ears. This is such a different view than Secretary Bryers's, who hopes to settle this diplomatically. Between you and me, he's actually meeting with Foreign Minister Yao in a private meeting right now. What do you suggest we do, specifically?"

Bannister smiled wolfishly. "I take it that you've seen the satellite images of their artificial islands. They're preparing for battle. Let's strike them from above: you should send planes and launch guided cruise missiles to attack their air bases on their islands. They might have amazing new nautical military technology, but on the islands, we can take them. We should decimate them. Leave nothing but ashes and blood."

"Let me think about it. I'm very sympathetic to your suggestion, but I mustn't be hasty. As usual, Bannister, you've piqued my interest. Stay safe over there."

Bannister knew not to push the president further. "I will. Thank you, Mr. President."

South China Sea

Alexei and Vika stood inside the control room of their Russian submarine, patiently awaiting orders. Although neither would admit it, they were extremely anxious.

"I do not like this," Alexei said after nearly an hour of silence. "We tell ourselves that we answer to no foreign power, yet here we are, awaiting orders from China."

"Don't worry so much," Vika replied. "Russia greatly benefits, too. In the end, our enemies will eat each other alive. And we get to personally punch the Americans in the nose. Enjoy it."

Anastasia pursed her lips. "Yeah, fine."

The conversation ended, and they once again stood in silence, waiting to receive their orders to launch torpedoes at U.S. carriers.

Washington, D.C.

United States National Security Director Adam Russell stood before the leadership members of Congress. The House and Senate leaders sat in the rounded rows of seats in the Speaker of the House's conference room, each eager to hear the latest about the seemingly impending war with China.

"Greetings," Adam began from the podium. "We have no time for pleasantries. What I tell you cannot leave this room. You all know the saying 'loose lips sink ships.' At this moment, war with China may be inevitable. Blood has been shed. I understand that there is disagreement in this room about what to do. We are up against a foe with evil intentions, and we will defeat them if necessary. The president is considering ordering an airstrike against the Chinese forces before they have a chance to attack us first."

Some of the congressmen rose from their seats and shouted, but their angry howls were incoherent to Adam.

"I understand that Secretary Bryers is still in China, negotiating a diplomatic solution," Senate majority leader Smith called above the mayhem. "We should give a peaceful resolution a chance."

"I think we need to strike quickly," Congressman Rodgers, the chair of the House of Representative's Defense Committee, retorted. "We need to gain a military advantage. We should attack first."

"The president is considering all options," Adam replied stoically. "We believe that this can be a quick victory. It won't be a long war."

"This will be a colossal mistake," Congresswoman Green, the minority leader of the House of Representatives, said loudly. "Once war begins, we may end up with an all-out nuclear war."

"Have faith," Adam said. "There will be no such thing."

White House, Washington, D.C.

"Mr. President," a Secret Service officer who had been assigned to protect the president said to him as he entered the Oval Office, "you need to come with me. Now."

The Secret Service officers escorted the president to an elevator that would bring them to the secured underground Presidential

Emergency Operations Center, which was a bunker structure under the East Wing of the White House.

The secretary of defense was already waiting by the elevator, looking calm but focused.

"Mr. President," one of the officers said. "The national security director will be right behind us."

"We're headed to the Presidential Emergency Operations Center for the remainder of this crisis," another Secret Service offer explained as they got out of the elevator.

After a few minutes of walking down the narrow tunnel, the guard reached a door. The president had to access the door through a facial recognition lock and via a code that changed daily. This code was carried by his military attaché.

The president looked inside the Presidential Emergency Operations Center as he entered it. There was a long wooden table, around which sat empty, black seats. Large computer screens and televisions hung on the far side of the room, but they were all turned off at the moment.

I can't believe I'm really here, and that we may have war, the president thought to himself. *It was built under F.D.R., in case there was ever an aerial assault on Washington. I guess there's something poetic about that, given the circumstances. At that time, the Germans were building rockets, and the Americans were rightfully concerned that they might attack the White House.*

If memory serves me well, President Truman went on to develop this bunker even further, turning into a bomb shelter.

This room was used on the September 11th attack on the World Trade Center. President Bush was actually in Florida when others in the White House fled to the bunker. The Secret Service had taken his family and other leaders down here for their protection.

And here I am.

I have everything I need to run a war just from this room.

"Mr. President," the security guard said, jolting the leader from his ponderings. "Military officers are on their way, as is the national security director, as I promised. Please, take a seat."

The president obeyed. Sure enough, about a dozen men and women quickly entered the room. Many of them sat around the table, while the military personnel stood on guard.

"Mr. President," the national security director said. "Congress has been apprised of your impending directives. Many were not pleased."

The president looked around at his colleagues, each waiting eagerly for his response.

This is my moment, he thought.

"Well, it's not up to them. But I should add that I have not given the order to attack China's artificial islands just yet. Bannister made a convincing case that I should, but ..."

"But what?" Adam asked politely.

"Something is nagging me," the president replied. "I can't explain it, but I want to wait a bit."

"Are you sure?" Adam asked. "I know Bannister, and I can imagine his arguments. Do you really want to risk waiting? A preemptive strike might be our best chance at victory. Fighting a war seven thousand miles away is always difficult. We need the element of a surprise first attack."

"I'm still very, very open to it," the president said. "But give it time. I understand the risk involved. But Adam, there is risk on all sides. Don't forget that Bryers is stuck in China with their foreign minister. Who knows—maybe he'll work a diplomatic miracle. He's always been a clever fox. If we don't receive any good news within three hours, then we'll do as Bannister would like. Until then, let us all go back to work in the command center."

Everyone obeyed the president's polite suggestion. Although he wore a confident mask, thoughts of doubt ran around in his head.

Three hours, he thought. *Please, God, don't let this have been the mistake of my life.*

Beijing, China

Minister Qiang sat in his office, studying a chart in front of him.

I need to coordinate our military response. Every minute counts. We have five departments: the Information Bureau, the International Communications Bureau, the Foreign Affairs Office, the Peacekeeping Office, and the Mobilization Office. I'll need to delegate tasks to the right people over the next few hours, if this situation escalates.

This is our time.

"Minister!" a panicked voice yelled.

Qiang looked up to see his favorite aide breathing so fast that Qiang thought he might faint.

"What is it, Bai?"

"The Americans look like they're about to enter our territory, even after we warned them not to!"

"Is our president in a safe location?"

"Yes, absolutely! He's in a secured control room."

Qiang rose to his feet. "I spoke with him half an hour ago. He wants to hear from Yao before giving any orders."

"Yao? But he's stuck with the Americans!"

"Exactly," Qiang said. "Remember, Bai, as an executive department under the State Council, we wield a lot of power. None of us can afford to make a mistake in times like this. We represent the Central Military Commission and the People's Liberation Army when engaging with the militaries of other nations.

"While we hold down the fort here, Yao might pull us from the brink. He is a good man."

"Well, in case otherwise, we need to prepare to attack first. It will give us a great military advantage. It may be the only we win."

TWENTY-SEVEN

★★★

CHAPTER

Yao and Bill both leaned forward, eagerly studying the map on the table.

"Okay," Yao said slowly, as his mind raced. Then, between nervous laughs, he said, "Well, at least we know what one of our problems is. The cartographers who drew the maps know that the United States and China disagree on where international waters begin and end. See how the English and Chinese versions of this map are vastly different."

Both men laughed.

"Right," Bill agreed. "It's a dispute over territory on the high seas. So far, so good. Got any ideas?"

Yao stared at the map as he traced his fingers across it. "Hmm … I'm embarrassed to say, nothing is coming to mind." He looked up hopefully at his American counterpart. "What do you think?"

Bill took a heavy breath. "I'm just working through the realpolitik that I know I'll have to deal with in Washington after my proposal. I asked my staff to prepare some possible settlements. It'll be tricky, but I think we can allow the current area that China claims off its main territory to remain under your authority … with conditions. This disputed territory, once placed in Chinese hands, will allow all commercial sea and air travel. Also, any commercial exploration of oil and gas will be shared proportionally with neighboring countries such as Japan, the Philippines, and Vietnam."

Yao smiled. "This cannot include our territory of Taiwan, or no deal."

"Fine."

"Okay, that's a start. I also have a briefing paper from my superiors. The agreement we've already come to will hardly stop the war, Secretary. What about our artificial islands?"

"Right, right. Okay, how about we allow China to claim the territorial sea around those reclaimed islands for twelve nautical miles, and in return, all international ships will be given a right to innocent passage according to the UNCLOS through the now-disputed Chinese seas."

Yao nodded. "That … should work. The U.S. Navy must obtain prior authorization before they enter the area."

"Yes, but there must not be any flybys."

"And you are suggesting that, beyond the twelve nautical miles, those waters will cease to be contiguous zone and exclusive economic zones? Will oil and gas rights go to the nearest country, rather than to our islands?"

"That's right," Bill said firmly.

Yao leaned back in his chair and thought about it for a while. "I cannot think of a reason why my superiors would be unhappy with that, given the current tensions."

Bill was feeling confident, but he knew his next point was going to be more challenging. "There will be no more harassment of U.S. Navy ships. Never again will there be an incident like the one that launched this crisis in the first place. All military flights—whether yours, ours, or anyone else's—must stay at least fifty nautical miles away from the U.S. Navy when in the South China Sea. This applies to both international waters and China's new territory."

Yao frowned as he thought over Bill's proposals. Finally, he said calmly, "Some of what you say makes full sense. Other pieces of your offer … I'm not so sure about. Do you mind if I consult with my staff?"

Bill nodded eagerly. "Of course. I'd tell you to take your time, but unfortunately we have no choice but to rush."

"Absolutely."

Bill smiled as he sat alone. *I got some of the settlement ideas from my Georgetown student Stewart's master's thesis. He will never know how important his paper was. It can never be revealed.*

Yao stood in a quiet hallway with four of his most trusted staff members, including Guo.

"The secretary of state and I are so close to reaching an agreement," Yao said softly. "But I need your thoughts."

"Sir, with all due respect, this seems to be a complete turnaround from our previous attempt at negotiating with the Americans," one delegate said. "Why the sudden hope for diplomacy?"

Yao knew he did not have time to be guarded, so he chose honesty without a second thought. "I earned Bill's trust by telling him about our nuclear-capable hypersonic missile, which is maneuverable and difficult to track and destroy. I think it caused him to understand just how serious war between China and the United States would be, and that they might not necessarily stop a nuclear war."

"You told him about our weaponry?" another staff member asked in shock. "Foreign Minister, that is treason!"

"We don't have time to argue over what is already done," Yao stated firmly. "We can deal with the political aftermath of my decisions later. For now, we have a war to stop. Now, may I hear your opinion on the secretary of state's deal?"

The four staff members nodded, although Yao noticed that they still looked disturbed.

"Good," Yao said. He then quickly ran through Bill's proposals.

"We only get twelve nautical miles around our islands?" one of the staff members asked. "No way. We need at least twenty-four. We would be giving up great mineral rights."

"Okay," Yao said. "I'll go back to Bryers with maybe forty or fifty and hope that he meets me in the middle. What else?"

"Are you sure you want to allow the United States Navy into our waters?" Guo asked skeptically. "That seems like a recipe for more conflict."

"What do you suggest as a compromise?" Yao asked.

"Try asking the secretary of state if he'd be willing to allow the U.S. Navy, but not its aircraft carriers, to enter the waters for innocent passage. That will reduce tensions."

Yao nodded gratefully. "I agree. I will negotiate. What else?"

The staff members remained silent, and Yao could see that they were conflicted.

"Hey," he snapped. "I appreciate your help. I know this is getting very dicey. I know that I may have crossed a moral line that makes you uneasy. Just stay strong for a little longer, and maybe the world won't witness World War III. Okay?"

They nodded obediently.

"Thank you," Yao said. "I'll talk to you again soon."

Yao returned to his seat across from Bill, who was sitting patiently with his hands in his lap.

"Your proposals are not unreasonable," Yao began in as friendly a tone as he could manage, "but I have a counteroffer. As you are well aware, any final settlement needs approval from our president."

Bill breathed a sigh of relief. *Thank God, peace is possible*, he thought to himself. "Same goes for us. Let's hear what you've got."

"First of all, we would like fifty nautical miles around our artificial islands."

Bill clasped his hands together and rested them on the table. "How about twenty, but you also have to commit not to make any more islands."

Yao stared at Bill with a tight, focused expression. "How about twenty-four, and we won't make more islands?"

Bill thought about it. "Will you allow for international shipping within those miles?"

"We can. But no more of your aircraft carriers in our territory."

"Okay," Bill said, "that's a deal."

Yao nodded. A rush of excitement coursed through him, but he kept himself in check. "I also want a hotline set up between our Departments of Defense, so that they can coordinate at all times."

"That's a good idea," Bill said with a smile. "No need to compromise on that front."

"Last thing," Yao said. "During the Cold War, the leaders of the United States and the Soviet Union had a hotline between each other's presidents, so that they could quickly resolve any issues without going to nuclear war. Our leaders should do the same."

"Two hotlines," Bill said teasingly. "Done."

"Wonderful," Yao said. "Do you have any other concerns?"

Bill rubbed his temple. After a long minute, he said, "No, actually. I am satisfied. We have ourselves a good settlement, in my opinion."

He reached his hand out, which Yao accepted.

"Thank you, Secretary," Yao said sincerely. "We will each have to run this plan by our respective leaders for approval. If they agree, we need to have a secret meeting with the United Nations Security Council. Then we will be well on our way. Once they agree to a meeting, all violence and brinksmanship will be ordered to a halt."

"Right. Neither I nor my superiors have the authority to simply give away what are now international waters. We need to contact all affected parties with claims to this territory for approval, too. We'll have to come together as an international community. This will take time. But to your point, now that we have a *potential* compromise, we can end the impending war. Or so I hope."

"We should make the calls now," Yao said without missing a beat.

"Yes. And if all goes well—that is, if our respective leaders at least agree to meet and discuss our proposals—we should have a celebratory toast tonight. Safe to say that we'll have deserved it."

Yao rose to his feet and smiled as widely as he had the day of his wedding. "I entirely agree."

"If you agree, we need to inform our militaries that a diplomatic agreement is close so that they do not fire on each other."

"I was thinking the same."

All of the diplomats and delegation stood in one of the large conference rooms. Josh and Guo had volunteered to help distribute champagne glasses to everyone.

"My friends!" Bill exclaimed, holding a glass of champagne up to the sky. "When we first arrived at this lodge, our negotiations went poorly. In fact, they were a disaster. But I now regard the snowstorm as something of a miracle. It's not an exaggeration to say that millions of lives have been saved by this one act of nature.

"Today, Minister Sheng and I both recognized that a diplomatic solution was the world's only hope. We put aside our differences, both cultural and personal, and came together. We knew that neither of us could possibly get everything that we wanted. But we also knew that a compromise was not just some ideal aspiration. We *had* to reach one. And so we did."

The diplomats murmured amongst themselves as the good news dawned on them. Then they clapped ferociously for a long while.

"Mr. Sheng and I will be happy to explain our resolution in greater detail during dinner or afterwards. Before we get back to work, I'd like to make a toast. To persistence, newfound friendship, and world peace!"

Bill and Yao raised their glasses, as did the rest of the crowd. The diplomats enjoyed their drinks in unison.

The two leaders looked at each other glowingly and shook hands once more.

"We really did it," Yao said in amazement. "Secretary, I—"

Yao abruptly fell into a coughing fit. After a few seconds, his drink fell from his hands, and he keeled over.

"Yao!" Bill cried and grabbed the foreign minister. "Yao, what's wrong?"

The foreign minister dropped to his knees and threw up violently.

The diplomats started noticing. The secretary of state sent for the doctors who had joined them on their trip, in case of health emergencies like this one. Many of the attendees panicked, while others rushed to where Bill stood above Yao.

As chaos swept through the dining hall, Josh sat back in his chair and took a nervous sip of his drink.

As soon as we were told about the toast, I knew Bannister would suspect the worst. And so of course he knocked on my door and told me to do the unthinkable—to slip the poison that I'd received before our trip into Yao's glass. It wasn't easy, sneaking my way into the lodge kitchen and making sure that I'd dosed the correct drink. Just before Guo handed the minister his drink, I slipped the poison into it. God, what am I becoming? Is all of this deception and destruction really worth it? But I'm in too deep now to change course.

The world had a chance to see peace between its two superpowers. What Yao and Bill managed to achieve is impressive, but it would have just given China time to grow stronger and, eventually, unstoppable. But no, I couldn't have that, either.

"Stop slouching," Bannister's voice whispered in Josh's ear.

The assistant secretary of state nearly jumped out of his seat.

Bannister smirked. "Look around you, Joshy boy. Look at them flailing. You did well. But you know what you still have to do."

"Get away from me," Josh whispered impotently.

Bannister rose to his feet and placed a condescending hand on Josh's shoulder. "So be it."

Just as Bannister walked away, a familiar voice called, "Josh! Are you okay? I don't understand what's happening!"

Josh looked up to see Guo, who was pale and shaking. "I don't know," he said quietly. "I guess someone didn't want the peace talks to finish on a good note."

"You're … you're so calm! Josh? What's wrong?"

Josh's eyes welled up. He looked down at Guo's shoes, as eye contact was impossible for him at the moment. "Nothing, Guo. Please, just leave me alone."

He felt her hand stroke his, but after a few seconds, it disappeared.

And Josh sat in utter solitude while Yao was taken away in an ambulance.

"Stop!" Bill yelled to the ambulance outside the lodge. "I insist I accompany the foreign minister!"

"No," a security aide said harshly.

Even in his confused state, Yao fumbled over to Bill, placed a hand on his shoulder, and said, "Please, don't leave me alone."

"I know where the hospital is," Guo said to the Chinese and American diplomats. "It'll be a difficult trip, especially in the snow. But the lodge has vehicles we can use. Who's coming with me?"

Every hand went up.

TWENTY-EIGHT
★ ★ ★
CHAPTER

B ill stood above Yao's unmoving body, staring at him as if trying to will the foreign minister back to consciousness. The medical team had placed Yao on a hospital bed and connected him to intravenous lines and monitors.

"Sir," a stern, feminine voice said from Bill's right. "I need to ask you to wait in the hallway for a few minutes."

"I won't leave his side."

"I will call you when we're finished here. Please, we need our space now."

Bill tore his head away and obeyed the woman.

In the hallway, he was surprised to see all of the delegates standing eagerly shoulder to shoulder. The U.S. and Chinese delegates were intermingled amongst each other, all with worried looks on their faces.

"Don't go in yet," Bill warned them.

"Secretary!" Josh said as he ran towards the front of the crowd. "Can I speak with you privately?"

Bill rubbed a worried hand over his face. "Yeah, Josh. Sure."

The two men walked down the hall until they were far out of earshot from everyone else.

"What's on your mind, Josh?" Bill asked quietly.

"I … I just wanted to see how you were holding up. It seemed like things were going well between you and the foreign minister. I'm here for you, boss."

Bill nodded gratefully. "Thank you, Josh. If you knew the things I had to do to earn Yao's trust, and now this …" He shook his head. "It might have all been for nothing."

Josh frowned. "What do you mean?"

Bill eyed the faraway crowd of delegates and pulled Josh closer towards him. "I knew that Yao and I didn't have much time. Our navy planned to cross China's red line in the South China Sea. If that had happened, war would've been inevitable. So I told Yao about our military's plans. I see the look on your face, I know—I committed treason. But it was the only way, Josh. I faced a hard choice. But dammit, I'd do it again tomorrow if it meant finding a peaceful solution."

"Secretary, I …"

"It's okay, you don't have to say anything. I understand if you think less of me. But please don't tell anyone else. If my decision gets out, it could cause strife within our ranks, and that's the last thing we need right now."

Josh took a wary step away from Bill. "Sure, boss. That's fine."

"Go be with the others. I'd like to be the first one Yao sees when he's up. In the meantime, I need to gather my thoughts, if you don't mind."

White House, Washington, D.C.

One of the president's aides, a young woman named Molly, entered the Presidential Emergency Operations Center, alongside two more Secret Service officers.

She nervously approached one of the empty seats at the table and stood in awkward silence.

"Molly," the president said seriously. "I assume you have important news to share. Please, sit."

She nodded and obeyed the president. "Mr. President, Yao Sheng has been poisoned."

Several people in the bunker audibly gasped, but the president remained calm.

"How is that possible?" he asked.

"I don't know," Molly said apologetically. "Apparently, Yao and our Secretary Bryers were about to celebrate their diplomatic compromise. Yao fell ill after they toasted glasses."

The president placed his chin on his fist. "My god. To think that we were on the verge of peace, and now this. We received news of their successful compromise, what, half an hour ago?"

"Mr. President," an older man at the table said, "we should contact Bannister."

"I know what he'll say," the president replied. "He'll suggest a first strike against the Chinese, before they blame us for Yao's poisoning."

"He's at the lodge," another woman said. "He can offer a perspective that we don't have."

The president thought in silence for a few seconds. Then he said, "So be it. Call him through the intercom, so we can all hear him."

After a few minutes, Bannister's disgruntled voice boomed throughout the bunker. "Hello?"

"Bannister," the president said. "What's happening?"

"You must've already heard," Bannister replied. "Yao's been poisoned. Everyone followed him to the medical room in the lodge. I stayed back. Had a feeling you'd call."

"Can you tell me anything I don't already know?"

"People were freaking out, last I saw. I think I know who did this—the Chinese military itself."

"What?" the president gasped. "That's a heavy charge, Bannister. What makes you think that?"

"You and I both know that the Chinese government never wanted a peace treaty. This is a false flag, covert operation. They ordered it so that they could accuse us of poisoning their foreign minister."

"Bannister, this is merely conjecture. How do you expect me to operate on such a flimsy accusation?"

"It's not flimsy," Bannister asserted impatiently. "Think about it. It gives them the perfect excuse to attack first and gain military advantage."

The president took a thoughtful breath. "What about Bryers? What is his status?"

"He's shaken, or at least he was last I saw him."

"Where is he now?"

"Probably with the others in the medical room, or near it. I went to my room just as they took Yao away."

The president tapped his finger on the table. "Bannister, I know you're a hawk, but I also value your opinion. What do you recommend?"

"Well, I know you won't attack just yet, but put our navy on high alert, at least. And be ready to bomb China's airfields before they strike us."

"Reasonable enough," the president said between sighs. "To think that I was on the cusp of pulling our forces back from the brink. Bannister, thank you. Be careful."

"Anytime, Mr. President."

"Alright," the president announced to the others in the bunker. "Contact all military officers in the South China Sea. Put them on high alert and ready to attack."

Beijing, China

Minister of National Defense General Shi Li pounded his fists on his desk.

Those cursed Americans, he thought as he seethed to himself. *I knew they couldn't put aside their pathetic egos for a compromise. They poisoned one of our greatest men. If he dies, I will make sure that they pay.*

Our first mistake was thinking that we could be diplomatic with the Americans in the first place. They started this mess, they intruded upon our territory. I was a fool to not speak up when we chose diplomacy in the first place. I won't make that mistake again.

America will pay for what it did to Yao Sheng.

Spratley Islands, South China Sea

"Our orders have changed," General Yichen told his commanders. "We are once again on high alert. Be ready for anything, including battle."

Yichen and his commanders were walking along the beach, headed towards their fleet of ships. Although the general did not say so, his commanders knew that they were on their way to man the ships and prepare for the worst.

"I don't understand," Zimo said. "Only an hour ago we were told to stand down."

"I don't know," Yichen admitted. "Earlier, I was told that Foreign Minister Sheng had reached some kind of deal with the Americans at their summit. But I wasn't told what changed. I'm not even sure our new orders have to do with the diplomatic efforts. But we must do as we're commanded."

"I don't like this," Zimo said nervously as they reached the dock. "Something feels off."

"Contain your emotions," Yichen responded harshly. "China needs you right now. Do not falter. We are ready to defeat the Americans."

Summit Lodge, China

Only a few seconds after Bannister hung up the phone, someone pounded on his door with three rapid knocks.

"Coming, coming!" he grunted.

Josh stood on the other side of the door, breathing fast and sweating as if it was the middle of summer.

"I have it."

Bannister frowned but pulled the young man inside his room.

"I just spoke with the president," Bannister explained as Josh paced back and forth. "Military's back on high alert. Don't let this get to your head, but you did well, kid. The poisoning worked."

"This is it," Josh said, as if Bannister had not said a word. "I give you this recording, and I'm finished! No more!"

"What? What recording?"

"I s-spoke with Bill. I got him on record admitting to treason."

Bannister opened and closed his mouth a few times before replying. "*What!* Why would he do such a thing? How? Josh ..." He laughed ecstatically. "You've done it! We'll have war on our hands in no time!" His laughter ended as his mind raced. "Josh, we need to leave China quickly. The storm has finally ended. I will send for a helicopter, and we can get to the airport and be out of here before the war begins."

"What about Bill and his team?" Josh asked.

"I don't care about those commie-loving bastards," Bannister spat.

Josh ran into the bathroom and closed the door.

Bannister laughed callously as the assistant secretary of state heaved and vomited.

The media will have a field day with this, Bannister thought. *And chaos will ensue.*

Bannister picked up his secured satellite phone and dialed a number that he knew by heart.

"Hello, this is Benny from Worldwide Newsroom," a cheery voice said.

"Benny, it's me," Bannister growled. "Give the phone to John."

"Ah, yes," Benny said nervously. "One moment, please."

"Hi, Bannister," a new, confident voice said. "I hear you're in China. How's the summit going?"

"Listen to me, John," Bannister whispered eagerly. "I got you the story of a lifetime. Bill Bryers committed treason. Listen to this tape."

Bannister played Josh's recording into his phone.

"Holy …" John gasped. "This is huge. So huge, in fact, that I need a second verification. Who recorded this?"

Bannister eyed the door to his bathroom. "Josh, the assistant secretary of state."

Suddenly, the vomiting sounds stopped, and Josh returned to Bannister's main room. Bannister beckoned the young man over. "Tell him what happened," Bannister commanded.

After Josh explained himself, John asked, "Can you send me a secure copy of the recording over the Internet?"

"Yeah, I can," Josh said softly.

Bannister tore the phone from Josh's hand and added, "And get this, John. The Chinese poisoned their own minister of foreign affairs as a false flag operation. There may be war."

"That's terrible," John said. "Get me that recording, and I'll get both stories out immediately."

Summit Lodge, China

"We've just finished pumping his stomach," one of the medics explained to Bill in the hallway. "He's currently being given intravenous fluids."

"Is he conscious?" Bill asked.

"Yes, though he's understandably tired. You're welcome to go in and see him, but please don't invite the others just yet."

Bill nodded and gestured to the rest of the delegates to wait patiently in the hallway. Then he followed the doctor to see Yao.

Bill smiled at his Chinese counterpart, who was already sitting up, despite the tubes connected to his arms.

"You look good," Bill muttered teasingly.

It took Yao a few moments to respond, but eventually he said slowly, "Secretary, I'm still kicking."

Bill laughed, walked closer to Yao, and delicately grabbed his hand. "I'm terribly sorry about this."

Yao opened his mouth to respond, but suddenly he fell into a violent coughing fit. The medics rushed over to him and pushed Bill out of the way.

"Sir, you need to leave us now."

As Bill stepped back, he asked, "Will he live?"

"Sir, please exit the room. Now."

Bill returned to the hallway in a disoriented daze.

He really could die. My partner—no, my friend—could die, and we could witness the bloodiest war in world history.

New York, New York

"In shocking news," Gina Garrett, news anchor for ABC News, began, "a recording of Secretary of State Bill Bryers has just been released to the public. As you know, Secretary Bryers has been leading a diplomatic engagement with the Chinese over the South China Sea debacle. Apparently, he had managed to reach an agreement with his Chinese counterpart, Foreign Minister Yao Sheng. But in doing so, he gave up military secrets and committed treason. Here is the recording."

"So I told Yao about our military's plans. I see the look on your face, I know—I committed treason. But it was the only way—"

"That's painful to hear," the other anchor, Tim Earlheart, said somberly. "I should note that the recording sounds like it cuts off midsentence, but the context is clear enough. Bill Bryers exposed government secrets to the Chinese in order to make a peace deal. Has he really committed treason?"

"I'm being told that both sides are once again on high alert," Gina said. "Apparently, there was a brief moment during which it seemed like leaders from both nations were open to accepting the peace deal that Bryers and Foreign Minister Sheng had agreed to. But in yet another twist, someone has poisoned Yao Sheng. It is unknown whether or not he will live. To our American viewers, we'd like to inform you that news stations around the world are also reporting on these strange events."

"An inside source has told us that the Chinese poisoned their own minister as an excuse for war," Tim said. "It is conceivable that this is a false flag operation. We will keep you, dear viewers, apprised of the situation. In the meantime, please stay calm, and stay safe."

Capitol Building, Washington, D.C.

"You need to fire Secretary Bryers!" Congressman Rodgers yelled into the phone. House and Senate leadership were having a conference call with the president. "He betrayed the United States! He is either a communist sympathizer or an idiot. Either way, he has ruined our chance at peace."

"I agree with Congressman Rodgers," Congresswoman Blackstone said. "This is a public relations disaster on a literal global scale. I checked my phone two minutes ago, and the editorials are already coming out. He needs to be returned home immediately, before war breaks out. If we have any last chance at peace, Bryers must not be anywhere near China."

"I say we throw him in jail!" Congressman Rodgers shouted angrily. "I don't care what happens to him after what he did. Maybe if we sacrifice him, China will take that as us waving the white flag, and we can keep the peace."

"Thank you, Mr. Speaker and majority leader," the president said. "I want to talk with Bill before I take any action. I hear that he is at the bedside of Minister Yao. Our military is on high alert. We could soon be at war with China."

"What a mess," Blackstone said. "I hope we do everything we can to avoid war."

The president sighed. "I am not sure that is possible."

TWENTY-NINE
★★★
CHAPTER

Moscow, Russia

van breathed down Anastasia's neck as she anxiously typed away on her keyboard.

This is it, he thought. *The West will collapse under its internal divisions, and China will be in our eternal debt.*

"Anastasia," he muttered quickly, "tell me the latest. But don't stop working."

"Okay," she said nervously. "We're flooding every social media platform with fake accounts, both American and Chinese. The goal is to confuse the Americans with disinformation and misinformation about Bill Bryers and Yao's poisoning. We created fake images to make it look like Bill poisoned Yao's drink. We also produced fake images that show the Chinese lodge staff doing it. We distorted that audio clip of Bill so it appears he's saying all sorts of contradictory messages. Bill has been on television many times in the past, so it wasn't difficult to generate false audio from the stock of previous recordings. Also, we are using social media to spread the word of Bill Bryers's treason so that Americans will distrust any last-minute diplomatic solution to the conflict between America and China."

"Total confusion," Ivan said with a grin. "Is it working?"

Anastasia nodded but never looked away from her computer screen. "According to my statistics tracker, hostile posts by Americans are up by over an order of magnitude since yesterday. Same goes for social media engagement. The Americans are angry, sir ... and at each other's throats."

"Excellent. You mentioned fake, contradictory messages from Bill. Could you play a couple for me? You may stop your other work to do so."

Anastasia hesitated, but after a pat on her shoulder by Ivan, she obeyed.

"Damn right, I poisoned that Chinese bastard. He thinks I'd just roll over and show my belly to him and his evil government? Oh, please. I came with a sword, not a white flag."

"Here's one more," Anastasia said.

"I betrayed the United States because China does everything better than us. I'm tired of pretending otherwise. What, you're going to hitch your wagon to a dying empire? You might think that's noble, but it's not. It's naïve."

"Impressive!" Ivan exclaimed. "I'll go see if riots have broken out in the United States yet. Good work, Anastasia."

White House, Washington, D.C.

The United States president watched the television screen in horror.

"As you can see," a local D.C. reporter said to the camera, "the previously peaceful protests have turned violent. Only an hour ago, factions were marching through the streets, each chanting its own message. Some carried signs with rather obscene language about Secretary of State Bill Bryers, others expressed hawkish views about China, and still others were anti-war. It was already a mess when two factions collided at a street corner and began tearing each other apart. I've been told that two protestors are confirmed dead."

The camera turned, and the president rubbed his temples as he watched the streets of the nation's capital fall to violent anarchy. The National Guard fell onto the scene, having been activated to address the chaos. Police were flooding the area, but even they appeared confused about who to target.

"This is a nightmare," the president said. "What can we do?"

"It's time to assume the worst-case scenario," the secretary of defense said soberly. "The good news is that these riots are usually short-lived. Let the police put a lid on the situation. The bad news is that the time for any kind of diplomacy is over.

"I expect that we will be attacked by the Chinese soon. We must launch our bombers to destroy multiple key targets."

"I am not ready to start a war," the president said angrily.

"Mr. President," the secretary of defense said carefully. "We can at least place the bombers in an air heading to the targets, so that we have options. You can always pull them back."

"Where the hell is Bryers?" the president said in frustration. "Find him. I need to speak with him."

"The Russians are manipulating our country," another high-ranking official added in order to change the subject. "I just checked social media. People are arguing about recently released images and audio recordings of Bill Bryers. A lot of them contradict each other, so people are taking stances on which are real and which are fake. It's madness."

The president nodded ruefully and turned the volume up on the television.

"I'm receiving word that over fifty thousand more protestors are arriving in Washington," the reporter continued. "Apparently, people have flown in from all over the country. We keep hearing reports of violent outbreaks."

The Pentagon

Joint Chiefs of Staff advisor Piya Agarwal eyed the art on the walls of the conference room.

Some of these paintings must be hundreds of years old, she thought. *Did the founding fathers feel the way I feel right now, back when they fought the British? And these flags that stand in this room … will the countries that they represent still stand by us after all is said and done?*

The Western democracies, as well as Japan, need to support us.

"Mrs. Agarwal," one of the military leaders said. "Thank you for your time. We need to discuss our plan of attack."

Piya snapped into focus without batting an eye. "Yes, Mr. Hughes. The president has ordered our long-range bombers into the air. They can refuel once they're off the ground."

"We can do that. Where, exactly?"

"Find out where our ships are in the South China Sea, and send the appropriate fighter cover. Use our bombers to destroy any Chinese naval vehicles in the war zone. This includes their three aircraft carriers, the air bases on their artificial islands, China's Atlantic naval base in Equatorial Guinea, and any Chinese invasion forces that may be launched towards Taiwan."

Beijing, China

Minister of National Defense General Shi Li sat confidently at the head of the Foreign Affairs Office's most private room.

A map of the South China Sea lay bare on the table. Li knew that the dots and marks on it were from earlier in the day, when he had met with high-ranking officials to discuss their strategies.

But now everything has changed, he thought grimly.

"This war may be beyond our control," he said to the military leaders sitting beside him. "We need to sink the Americans' aircraft carriers first with hypersonic missiles."

"This is very doable," the man to Li's right said. "Russia has assured us that they can keep the Americans' submarines engaged in battle long enough to divert their attention. They don't have the resources to attack our fleet."

Li nodded. "Good. Send the message down all lines of communication to our men and women on the high seas. If war erupts, target the aircraft carriers first."

Kadena Air Base, Okinawa, Japan

The young Akiko watched with his arms crossed as fighter jets flew into the skies above the Pacific waters.

"Now is the time," his older colleague, Kenta, said quietly. "Taiwan cannot defend herself right now. We need to help defend her against China."

"What about our navy?" Akiko asked.

"They are on high alert and also headed towards Taiwan. Naval ships are on their way to the seas between China and Taiwan to serve as deterrence. But that is merely one theater of many, as you know."

Akiko bowed his head. "South Korea could be the bloodiest theater of them all."

"Indeed. Our forces are on their way as we speak. They will join the hundred thousand or so American troops already in South Korea. Our men and women will act as a reserve in case North Korea crosses the demilitarized zone."

"I knew our prime minister wanted to display his strength," Akiko began, "but I'm still surprised at the readiness with which he is joining the fray."

Kenta put a fatherly hand on Akiko's back. "Our foreign minister had a fruitful meeting with his American counterpart just the other month about our alliance against the Chinese. Japan doesn't forget its allies when they need her most. And now is most certainly a time of need."

Korean Demilitarized Zone

Jung Pak stood behind her partner's armored truck as if it was a shield. When she had first joined the Republic of Korea's armed forces, she knew that a day such as this one was always a possibility, but part of her had hoped it would never come to this.

Yet there she was, facing off against the Communist Korean People's Army. She stood in the middle of an ocean of South Korean troops. All of the nation's reserves and overseas soldiers had been ordered to the demilitarized zone in anticipation of aggression by the North Koreans.

On our side, there is such beautiful greenery, she thought to herself. *Across the demilitarized zone in North Korea, all of the trees are gone, used up for firewood. In their place are just barren hills. Rolling green hills on the one hand, and threatening barbed wire fences on the other.*

Our political leaders were right to bring in the troops, she thought as she eyed the North Korean soldiers in the distance. *Thank goodness we discovered their tunnels that can carry tens of thousands of troops per hour into our country. I can only pray that there are no more secret tunnels that North Korea dug that we failed to find. That would be a disaster.*

I remember learning about the history of the demilitarized zone as a young girl. The infamous 38th parallel north, the border between the United States' and Soviet Union's dominions. Ever since the end of World War II, this region has been fraught with tension. Some think that things calmed down after the Cold War, but I know better.

The Korean War was brutal. Our enemies to the north crossed the 38th parallel on June 25th, 1950. Three million people died. North Korea had Chinese and Russian support, while the United States led a United Nations–sanctioned army. Only in 1953 was this DMZ officially established via the Armistice Agreement. A buffer between their troops and ours, two hundred and fifty kilometers long and four kilometers wide. It was never enough.

Even before today, there has been the occasional burst of violence. Since the Korean War, over five hundred of our soldiers have died in this dark no-man's-land. Every one of those should have been a wake-up call to our political leaders. But they never found it urgent enough to do anything about the DMZ's fragility, and here we are.

Jung looked into the distance at the North Korean military. Like her, they were mostly still.

But she knew how quickly silence could turn to chaos.

North Korean side of the Demilitarized Zone

Hundreds of thousands of troops and numerous groups of tanks were assembling.

"We are ordered to strike Seoul if war breaks out," a general in uniform with dozens of medals said to nearby military troops. "As head of the artillery company, I will not disappoint our great leader.

The enemy's capital is only twenty-three kilometers away. We can rip it to shreds in an instant."

South China Sea

Admiral Dungy waited until he held the attention of all of the commanders aboard his ship. As soon as the cabin was utterly silent, he said, "We have crossed China's red line. Our orders now are to retaliate in full force if we are attacked. We are *not* to initiate aggression from this point onwards. Is everyone clear on that?"

He waited for everyone's nod of approval.

"Good. Now, let's review our battle plans in the event that we are attacked. If Chinese ships come for us, we will use the bombers to hit their airfields and our cruise missiles to sink their ships. Are we clear?"

The commanders nodded once again.

Chinese Naval Base, Equatorial Guinea, Africa

"We established your new military base in Africa just in time, it seems," the minister of defense said over the phone.

"Indeed," Officer Dao replied. "Even if, for whatever reason, the Americans wanted to try something sneaky over the Atlantic Ocean, they have us to contend with."

"Your warships are at the ready, I presume?"

"Absolutely. We can go on the offensive, too, whenever you want."

"Thank you, Dao. But let's not rush to attack the American ships just yet."

"We'll be here, ready for your command. What's the latest in the South China Sea?"

"I was told only minutes ago that Russian anti-submarine technology has set its attention on any incoming American submarines. The Russians have deployed two ships in particular from their northern fleet: the *Omega* and the *Naryan*. They will track, attack, and destroy American submarines at a moment's notice."

Dao smiled. "I'm feeling confident, sir."

"So am I, old friend. So am I."

Camp Lemmonier, Djibouti, Africa

"Our bombers are on high alert," Lieutenant Churchman said to his friend Lieutenant McNamara in the dining hall of their encampment. "They're headed to Equatorial Guinea as we speak."

"You mean they're going to stand off against China's navy over there?"

"Yep. It'll take hours to arrive, but we can't underestimate their presence in Africa. China has military footholds across the world at this point. We need to meet them everywhere they are, not just in the Pacific."

"Nowhere is safe," McNamara said. "This is getting wild."

"If we go to war with China, then we cannot allow them to operate from a naval base in the Atlantic. They'd be able to attack us directly from it, and they could expand the war to Europe or even mainland United States."

London, England

"It'll read 'World at War?' across the screen after the commercial break," a voice said in Hilary's ear.

"With a question mark?" Hilary asked quietly and quickly.

"Yes."

"Okay, good."

"The professor is standing by. He's ready for the video interview. You have ten seconds."

Hilary took a deep breath and brushed aside any feelings of panic that she had about the state of the world.

Things are happening so fast, but I need to stay calm, objective, and lucid in moments precisely like these, she thought.

"Welcome back to BBC News," she said, as a screen before her lit up with the face of an older, bearded man. "I'm here on live video with Oxford University professor of military history Edmund Tannett. Dr. Tannett, thank you so much for your time."

"Thank you, Hilary."

"Let's talk about what's on everyone's minds. Do you see parallels between the current geopolitical crisis and any other moments in world history?"

"I do, Hilary. You see, right now we have China and the United States on the brink of total war over essentially a minor dispute in the South China Sea. Their allies have been drawn into the fold as well. And so, a single unfortunate event may spawn a world war, the likes of which we haven't seen in nearly a century. It's very reminiscent of World War I. At that time, nationalism swept over Europe, and rational decision-making fell to the wayside.

"There's another parallel now, too. Most people know that World War I was kicked off because of the assassination of a single political figure. And look at what just happened: someone tried to kill China's foreign minister! The similarity is almost eerie."

"I was thinking the same thing as you spoke. History really does tend to repeat itself. Now, I want to get back to something you said: Do you think that nationalism is the problem now?"

The professor paused before responding. "You know, Hilary, I'm not so sure nationalism is the problem this time around. We live in a far more interconnected world today. In a way, free trade has resolved some issues of nationalism. After all, trading partners have an incentive not to go to war. Rather, the issue today is simply power politics. We have an emerging power in China eager to supersede an established power in the United States on the world stage. To be clear, I don't mean to only blame China. This is simply the game theory of the situation."

"It sounds like war between these superpowers is inevitable, then," Hilary said.

"Well, we should never discount the miracle that is diplomacy," Dr. Tannett replied. "But I fear that that ship has sailed, given the shocking news about Bill Bryers, as well as the attack on Yao Sheng."

"Do you see any hope for peace?"

"To be frank, it seems unlikely at this stage," the professor said soberly. "But I will offer this silver lining: throughout history, mankind has delivered miracles in the face of extraordinary adversity. I have concluded that human ingenuity is not predictable—we have often risen to the occasion. So if there is any chance that we can avoid war, it will be due to human ingenuity. I wish I could offer something more concrete than that, Hilary."

"I understand, and I appreciate your honesty. Let us hope that someone, somewhere can stop this insanity and help us avoid World War III."

White House, Washington, D.C.

"Mr. President," an officer said in the presidential bunker, "the chairman of the Joint Chiefs of Staff is on the line. Shall I video him in?"

"Yes, please," the president responded.

The chairman appeared on the largest screen in the bunker. Although he was dressed in a uniform that was decorated with medals, his face was pale and haggard.

"Mr. Chairman, much has happened since we last spoke."

"Indeed," the chairman replied. "We stand ready to counter any attacks by China or her allies. What are your orders with respect to Taiwan?"

The president frowned. "Why are you asking about Taiwan now?"

"China has moved troops towards her coast. The latest reports indicate that transport boats are settling there in preparation to invade."

The president rubbed his temples. *This is quickly spinning out of my control.*

"We are bound to defend Taiwan," he said after a few seconds. "We have verbal defense agreements with her leaders. Do everything that you must in order to protect Taiwan."

"I will deliver the order, Mr. President. Does this include both the navy and the air force?"

"Absolutely. With luck, China will appreciate our firepower and stand down. Godspeed, chairman."

THIRTY
★ ★ ★
CHAPTER

Hi, Mr. Bryers?" a doctor said to Bill, who stood alone just outside the makeshift hospital unit.

"Yes," Bill replied eagerly. "How is Yao?"

"He's still unconscious, but there are signs that he'll survive."

"Oh, thank God. Can I see him again?"

The doctor shook his head. "Not just yet, but I didn't want you worrying anymore. Nothing is guaranteed, but at this moment, it looks like Yao will make it. I'll return once we have more news. Maybe get yourself some food and water. If I may say so, you look a bit bleary-eyed."

The doctor shook Bill's outstretched hand. "I appreciate the advice. Thank you, doctor."

"I'm happy to serve."

Bill was left alone once more. He closed his tired eyes. The secretary of state was weary and distraught.

I've come to really care about Yao. He and I developed a close friendship. His death will certainly result in war.

After several minutes of silence, someone said in a deep voice, "Secretary Bryers."

Bill opened his eyes and quickly composed himself. Before him stood a tall, fit man with buzzed red hair. His expression was so serious and still that Bill may have mistaken him for a mannequin had he not already known who he was.

"Taylor," Bill said. "What is the CIA station chief doing here? Surely you have more productive things to do than check on the foreign minister's health."

"I'm here to speak with you, Bill. I'm guessing you haven't been following the news?"

The secretary of state shook his head.

"Got it. Things have gone very badly for you. Tapes have been released to the world of your admission to treason. More than that, some of the tapes contradict each other, so no one quite knows what to believe. But all of them paint you in a horrible light. The president wants to talk to you before any criminal action for treason is brought against you."

Bill blinked. He did not have any more emotional energy to spend on this shocking news.

I'm going to jail, aren't I? Everything that I've worked for, the greatest purpose of my life besides my family, is about to go up in flames. Was it worth it?

"There's more," Taylor continued. "We have reason to suspect that John Bannister and Josh Thompson are guilty of poisoning Yao. Witnesses saw Josh tamper with Yao's drink, and the two of them apparently fled."

Bill frowned. "What? No, they'd never do that ..."

The secretary of state thought back to his last conversation with Josh.

I told him that I had committed treason for the greater good. Was he recording me? Why would he do that? I've always been good to Josh, ever since he was a young man.

Could he really have poisoned Yao, too? Bannister would ... maybe. But not Josh. Or am I naïve?

"Secretary, it's looking very likely that the two of them are guilty. I cannot get into why we suspect them at this moment, but rest assured that justice will be delivered. And before you ask, it appears that they have fled the lodge. Presumably, they will be outside of Chinese borders very soon."

So much is happening, so quickly, Bill thought. *I can hardly keep the moving pieces straight.*

"Where does that leave us?" Bill asked. "What's the latest on the impending war with China?"

"Secretary, I fought in Iraq. Like you, I never want the United States to go to war again. The costs have grown too high. But Bannister does not think like us. In particular, he's never been a fan of intelligence agencies. He thinks that we are too dovish, too cowardly. He prefers swords over words. But he fails to understand that if we actually fought with China, our best hope would be a quick war. Anything longer than, say, a few days would end in disaster, regardless of the winner. Bannister doesn't realize that the age of global warfare is over."

"It has to be," Bill said quietly. "War between empires risks human extinction now."

"Especially between *these* empires," Taylor agreed. "China has 2.2 million troops to our 1.4 million. Their navy has more ships than ours, although ours is still more powerful. And we have eleven aircraft carriers to their three. It would be a brutal, internecine fight." Taylor sighed heavily. "We're closer to war with China than we've ever been. We just launched our bomber jets. They're on their way to their potential targets as we speak."

Bill placed his face in his hands. "No, no. My god, Taylor. There has to be something I can do."

"I'm sorry, Bill. Between Yao's current state and the heat on your reputation following the tapes, you're a sitting duck."

Bill clenched his jaw and suddenly stood tall. "Yao will wake up. And when he does, the two of us will stop this war. He and I were so close. We can do it, Taylor. Just have a little faith."

"It's not you I doubt," Taylor replied. "You're the most talented diplomat I've ever met. But even you can't stop the clock from ticking."

"Yes, Mr. President," Guo said quietly into the phone. "I will ask the doctors to wake him up immediately."

Guo hung up the phone and left the private conference room. She walked silently through the crowd of Chinese and American diplomats and into the room in which the caretakers were looking after Yao.

"You can't be in here," a woman in a white coat said to her.

Guo shook her head. "I was just on the phone with the president. He insists that you wake Yao up now."

"That would be irresponsible," the doctor replied. "Yao looks to be recovering slowly, but forcing him to wake up could put his life at risk."

"I understand, but I know the foreign minister. If it was for the good of China, then he would risk his life. Please, doctor."

"His body is still in shock. He needs sleep in order to heal properly."

"The president demands that he speak with Yao. Please, I'm begging you. Yao would want to do this."

The other doctors began to take notice of Guo, and they all turned to her. They murmured amongst each other as Guo stood idly before them.

"We will slowly try to wake him," the female doctor said reluctantly. "There are no guarantees that this will work. He could die, but if the president ordered it, so be it."

Guo bowed her head. "Thank you very much. You have nothing to worry about. Yao is a survivor."

"I pray that you are right."

Beijing, China

Director of the Ministry of State Security Fai Wang sat at his shiny wooden desk in thoughtful silence.

The MSS is meant to secure China against foreign spies and domestic counterrevolutionaries, he thought. *We've held the line so far—the American intelligence agencies are not as powerful as they believe themselves to be. But can I prevent them from sabotaging us in an all-out war?*

We've certainly done our job well in recent years. I'm proud of my team for capturing six bloggers for slandering our soldiers a few months ago. Those vile writers said that we lied about the number of innocent people who died in a recent geopolitical skirmish.

But we've had our troubles with Western powers. Earlier this year, England banished three of our agents who were masquerading as journalists. But I suppose that was nothing compared to the American leviathan that we now face.

Fai's office door opened, and three men walked into the office with deliberate steps. Fai recognized all of them as his subordinates.

"What is it?" he asked.

"Sir," one of them said as they approached his desk, "we have evidence that the Americans poisoned our beloved minister. Several witnesses saw the United States assistant secretary of state handle the drink that was given to Yao Sheng."

Fai sat tall in his seat, suddenly jolted into focus. "How confident are you in these witnesses' testimonies?"

"Quite. The details of their stories are consistent with one another."

"Where is this assistant now?"

The subordinates shifted nervously. "He appears to have fled the country, along with his presumed accomplice, National Security Advisor John Bannister."

"Put out an arrest warrant for both of them," Fai commanded.

"But, sir, they are most likely no longer in the country."

"I don't care," Fai replied. "Let the world know that China demands justice for what they did. Think about it. We'll tell the media. They will do our bidding for us: they will explain the situation, and millions of viewers will recognize the United States as the villain that she is."

"Alright, sir. Consider it done."

London, England

"The next headline will read 'World on the Verge of War,'" a voice said in Hilary's ear.

"Okay," she replied with hesitation. "Are you sure we're not fearmongering at this point?"

"Definitely not. You've seen the footage. How can you possibly think that?"

"I'm just trying to think of all angles," Hilary said defensively. "But okay, I won't fight you on this."

"Live in three seconds. Two, one ..."

"Hello, and welcome back to BBC News. Tensions between China and the United States are at an all-time high. In the latest chapter of this saga, both American and Chinese intelligence agencies have come to suspect two Americans of poisoning Chinese foreign minister Yao Sheng. Multiple eyewitness accounts have corroborated the accusation. Meanwhile, China has demanded their arrest. Paul, who are these two Americans?"

"One of them is the assistant secretary of state, Josh Thompson. Hilary, this is a shocking development. Not only is Secretary of State Bill Bryers suspected of treason, but now his assistant is thought to have poisoned China's foreign minister! The other American is National Security Advisor John Bannister. Apparently, he has a reputation for being extremely hawkish on China. But to take it this far is ... Hilary, I don't have words. How can the United States possibly claim the moral high ground anymore?"

"It's an important question," Hilary replied. "The geopolitical ramifications will be enormous. And I'm not just talking about impending war. At this point, the United States may lose the support of her allies."

"Now *that* would be an interesting development," Paul said. "Experts are divided on who would win in a war between China and the United States. But the question answers itself if America loses her allies. Frankly, the United States would have no choice but to bend to China's demands."

"It would be the most significant moment in this century," Hilary said. "Paul, do you see any way out of this mess?"

"We hear that Foreign Minister Yao and Secretary of State Bryers worked out a peace settlement. If the minister and the Americans promise justice against the assassins, then there is still a possibility for peace."

"I'm not even sure there's time for that," Hilary said. "We have reports from across the world that militaries are ready to go to war. We couldn't be closer to a World War III scenario. But you're saying there's still hope?"

"I've been a reporter for a long time. I've seen good situations turn badly and vice versa more times than I can count. When it comes to human beings, there are always surprises. Until war actually begins, there is hope for peace."

THIRTY-ONE
★★ ★
CHAPTER

Washington, D.C.

"Mr. President," the secretary of defense said, "it's time. The bomber planes need a 'go' or a 'no-go.' Landing crafts are leaving China for Taiwan. We must launch air strikes on these landing crafts, the artificial islands, and the Chinese Navy. Chinese missiles have already shot down two of our military satellites. Some of our GPS systems have been damaged, so our cruise missiles may no longer be reliable."

The president eyed the nearby television screen, where Bannister had connected via video from inside an airplane.

"Bannister, you're suspected of having poisoned Yao Sheng. Witnesses claim to have seen Josh inserting poison into the foreign minister's drink. And now you're on the run. None of this looks good for you or me. But your advice is sound. What do you think I should do?"

Bannister grunted. "I know they're looking for me. Everything will be fine, Mr. President. The boy and I ran, but we're innocent. China is trying to make us look guilty. And anyway, China will be dead in the water before she can do anything to me or Josh. As for what to do, I've told you already: attack first, before China does."

"Thank you, Bannister," the president said. "I believe that you're innocent. The Chinese are probably just trying to foment division and animosity among us. Good luck to you."

The television screen went black.

"Please someone put Bill Bryers on the line. I understand he doesn't have a cell phone with him. I can wait."

After a few minutes, Bill's voice came through the intercom. "Mr. President?"

"Secretary Bryers," the president said angrily. "These tapes … are any of them true?"

There was a long pause before Bill responded. "I did commit treason, sir. I told them of our intent to cross the red line. I did it to create a sense of urgency, so that Yao would be more motivated to work with me and find a diplomatic solution. I'm terribly sorry, but world peace was at stake."

"I'm disappointed, Secretary. You know that you'll have to resign. A trial is in order, too. I'll always appreciate everything you've done for the United States of America, but your life is about to radically change for the worse."

"I understand, Mr. President. I won't beg for clemency."

"I wouldn't expect you to. I know you had your reasons, but you can give your reasons to the court. Meanwhile, you can still do good before the day ends. How is Yao Sheng?"

"He's in and out of consciousness but very likely to survive. Mr. President, we cannot wage a war with China. It wouldn't just be a limited skirmish. It'd be another world war. Yao and I had come to a fair settlement through diplomacy. Surely we can bring that to the world's powers for approval."

The president leaned back in his chair and closed his eyes.

"Hello?" Bill asked after several seconds of silence. "Mr. President?"

Finally, the president said, "Take care of yourself, Mr. Bryers."

Beijing, China

The president's lead advisor paced back and forth in the command center, flailing his arms wildly as he spoke. "We must attack the Americans, Mr. President! And now, before they strike first. You've seen the satellite images of fighter bombers heading towards us. They will reach us in thirty minutes."

"Calm down," the president said. "The rest of your team is on the other side of the door. I don't want them hearing this. Not yet, anyway. What's the latest on Yao?"

"I was told that he is still unconscious, although he is likely to live."

The president pounded a fist on his desk. "I need to speak with him!"

"Mr. President …"

"What? Do not doubt me. Call Guo and have her tell the medics to wake Yao up."

The advisor nodded nervously. "Yes, sir."

"Good. Also, prepare to launch a strike against the American navy that crossed into our territory. Get it done."

Summit Lodge, China

"No," Yao muttered weakly to the nearest doctor. "I'm dazed enough, I don't want any medications."

Bill stood by his counterpart's side with a hand delicately on Yao's shoulder. "Yao, are you sure you're okay with being awake?"

The foreign minister smiled faintly. "My president wants to speak with me, so yes."

"If you say so," Bill replied with a smile. "Yao, I also have to call my president back. But I want you to know that I'm glad you're okay."

Yao managed to place a weak hand over Bill's. "Thank you, my friend. I don't blame you for what happened to me. I trust you."

Bill nodded and left the room. He walked all the way back to his suite, picked up the phone, and dialed a number that he had memorized.

In a moment of clarity, he realized that he needed to use a more secure phone. He dropped the phone, picked up his secret, secret phone, and redialed.

"Hello?" a tired voice said from the other end.

"Mr. President, it's me again. Listen, Yao is alive and well. He'll be speaking with his own president shortly."

"Oh, thank God."

"I believe he was poisoned by Bannister and Josh."

"No!" the president yelled indignantly. "I already spoke with Bannister. He would never do such a thing."

"I know how you feel. I thought the same thing about Josh. I'm sorry, Mr. President, but all of the evidence points to them."

"What would you have me do, Bill?"

"The right thing. Have them arrested and put on trial. I'm willing to face the music for what I've done. Let them do the same."

"You think that will bring peace?" the president asked skeptically.

"I think we have to try. Remember, forty million people died in World War I. Around double that died in World War II. Imagine the death toll of what would be World War III if we end up fighting China. It's unacceptable, sir. Yao and I already had a diplomatic solution in place. Neither side will be completely satisfied with our compromises, but the solution works."

"I'm not sure the international community is still open to your proposal," the president said.

"Why not try?" Bill asked desperately. "Look, I know this is the end of my career. I did what I did for the sake of peace and diplomacy. Throughout history, diplomats have always been the unsung heroes of civilization. Military leaders receive all the glory, but diplomats are the ones who broker peace. We shuttle back and forth between warring parties in order to resolve bloody conflicts. It's what I've done my entire career. I'm honored that I've been in such a noble position. I'll walk into court with my head held high. Let them decide what my punishment should be. I'll still sleep well at night, knowing that I did everything in my power to save millions or billions of lives."

"I understand, Bill," the president said empathetically. "You're not the bad guy. I'll always be grateful for your service. Let me consider your suggestion. Maybe there's a chance that I can connect with China's leaders and rekindle our hope for a diplomatic solution."

"Thank you, Mr. President."

Bill hung up the phone and wiped a tear from his eye.

It's really over for me, after all these years.

He slowly walked back to the makeshift emergency room.

"Bill!" Yao said joyously from his bed. "Did you speak with your president yet?"

Bill walked over to the foreign minister and took his hand. "Yes, I did. You?"

Yao nodded. "I reminded him of the solution that you and I came up with."

"I did the same."

"I reminded my president that both his parents and mine had witnessed the devastation that war can bring. China's battle with Japan remains in our collective memory. I also told him that wars never go as planned—they often end up bloodier than people had anticipated."

"And that worked?" Bill asked.

"It seemed to give him pause," Yao said quietly. "I don't know what he'll decide."

"What now, Yao? And how are you feeling?"

The foreign minister shrugged. "I'm in a good mood, knowing that we've done all that we can, Bill. I suppose now we all just go home."

Bill frowned. "Can I stay until you're fully recovered?"

"That's very thoughtful of you, but it would be too dangerous for you to stay in China. The medical staff has done a great job here. I'll be fine."

"You really do care about your people, don't you?" Bill asked.

"I almost retired," Yao said. "Just as the tragedy on the South China Sea happened, I was ready to submit my resignation letter. But I'm glad I chose to help my beloved China one last time. If nothing else, I made a new best friend."

"This could be the last time we see each other," Bill said solemnly. "I could be spending the rest of my life behind bars for what I did."

"Oh, Bill. Is there anything I can do?"

Bill's eyes welled up again. "No, Yao. Just live your life. Your wife is looking down on you with pride."

"And your family knows that you were righteous," Yao replied. "Thank you, friend."

Both men silently stared at each other for a long time, not knowing if there would be war or peace. Tears fell, but neither man bothered to wipe them away.

THIRTY-TWO
★★
CHAPTER

Two Years Later

Yao sat at his home office desk, idly reading articles on his computer.

Knock, knock.

"Yes?" he called without looking up.

The door creaked open, and his personal assistant entered the office. "Hello, sir."

Yao turned away from his computer and made eye contact with his assistant. "Hi. Is everything alright?"

"Oh, yes. Your driver is waiting for you."

Yao frowned and looked at his watch. "Ah!" he cried. "The time went by so quickly. Thank you for alerting me."

Yao quickly threw on his nicest suit jacket and ran out of his house into the crisp autumn air, desperate not to be late.

As he approached the car, the passenger window descended, revealing the face of a beaming young woman.

"Ju!" Yao shouted excitedly. "What are you doing here?"

"I thought I'd keep you company, Dad. I don't know when you'll be back from your trip to America."

Yao jumped into the car and hugged his daughter. "I won't be gone for long, my love."

"What if there's a blizzard in Washington, D.C.?" Ju joked.

Yao laughed. "I'll be fine, I promise. We'll spend a whole weekend together as soon as I return."

Ju's expression suddenly became somber. "Are you looking forward to seeing Mr. Bryers?"

Yao's lower lip trembled, but he refused to break down in front of his daughter. "I most certainly am."

Washington, D.C.

Yao was surprised by how nervous he was, as he stood at the Dulles airport terminal in Washington.

Will they hate me? he wondered.

"Mr. Sheng?" a tall woman with curly blonde hair said.

Yao eyed her for a moment before extending his hand. "Please, call me Yao. And you must be Sloan. It's a pleasure to meet you."

Yao eyed the younger woman next to Sloan, who looked so much like Bill. She was holding the hands of two young boys. Yao guessed that they were around three and five years old.

"And you must be Gabrielle."

"Hello, Yao," Gabrielle replied. "I've heard wonderful things about you."

"Hi," the five-year-old said sheepishly.

Yao smiled, leaned down, and patted the boy on the head. "Hi! What's your name?"

"Bill," he said.

Yao's eyes widened as he rose to his feet. "Was he …?"

"Yes," Gabrielle answered. "He was named after my dad."

They all stood in awkward, emotional silence for a few heavy moments.

"The car is waiting for us," Sloan said. "Yao, are you ready?"

Yao held his head high. "Yes."

The five of them walked together out of the airport and entered a large, black car.

Yao placed his shaking hands in his pockets so that no one would see them.

"Were you friends with Grandpa?" Bill asked minutes into the drive.

Yao turned and forced a smile as he looked down at the boy's cherubic face. "I was. He was the greatest man I ever knew."

"He was? What did he do?"

Yao glanced at Gabrielle, who lightly shook her head.

"Maybe your mom can tell you all about his adventures one day," Yao said. "But I can say that he chose the righteous path, even when he knew it would cost him."

"Oh," the boy said, confused. "Okay."

"We're here," Sloan said.

They exited the car and approached what Yao knew was Arlington National Cemetery. His eyes watered as he took in its lush greenery. In the distance, lumbering trees of every red and green shade gave cover to the innumerable white tombstones across the massive field.

"I know where to go," Sloan said. "Follow me."

They walked for a minute or so until they found a particular tombstone, an exact copy of all the rest except for the letters on its face.

Yao read them and audibly cried.

Gabrielle's three-year-old son took Yao's hand.

"I miss you, Dad," Gabrielle said to the tombstone. "We all do. My kids are good. Mom is good. We're all so proud of you. Oh, and we brought an old friend of yours."

The aide that had accompanied them set up a few chairs for them to sit in.

Yao waved at the tombstone. "Hi, Bill. I'm sorry I didn't bring a drink for you—I would've toasted your memory. I miss you so much, my dear friend. In only seventy-two hours, we went from enemies to best friends. I learned more from you during that time than from any of the diplomats I've met in my life. Because of you, I know that life is nothing without a higher purpose. Because of you, I know that sacrifice is more noble than retaining one's pride. I love you, Bill."

Yao wiped the tears from his face before continuing. "You never told me that you were dying, even while we worked together at the summit. It was only four months later that you died. Exactly one hundred and twenty days after we went our separate ways, you left this earth. Dammit, I wish you had told me that you were sick.

"I've never known someone as dedicated to peace as you were. You committed treason against your own beloved country in order to avoid a tragic war.

"I know that we are brothers in spirit and soul. My dear, dear friend, you will be greatly missed."

Yao closed his eyes and breathed in the cemetery's cool air. He heard Bill's loved ones sobbing, but he knew that his pain was different from theirs.

My bond with Bill was like none I've ever had with anyone else.

Eventually, they rose from their chairs and slowly strolled around the cemetery, silently enjoying each other's company under such dark circumstances.

"What will you do now, Yao?" Sloan asked.

Yao placed a friendly hand on her back. "Spend time with my family. You know, I nearly retired, just before the incident on the South China Sea. I still could have, but my country needed me."

"So you almost never met Bill?"

"That's right. I don't know if you believe in fate, Sloan, but I do, now more than ever. I'm so sorry that Bill was sick. But I thank the heavens every day that I had the honor of knowing him."

Sloan took Yao's hand, and together they finished their walk.

ABOUT THE BOOK

As Commander Wong gazes into the vastness of the South China Sea from the deck of a Chinese Navy ship, he is alerted that a US Navy battleship is approaching. Meanwhile as Admiral Smith stands in the control room of the US battleship, three Chinese jets fly overhead and warn the crew that they are in foreign waters. But neither leader has any idea that in mere seconds, everything is about to change.

After a computer glitch prompts a US Navy lieutenant to make a split-second decision to take down two of the Chinese aircraft with missiles, the Chinese retaliate and launch their own attack. While Russia and others push China toward war, a peace summit is called. But can the sworn enemies who are leading the summit find a way to utilize diplomacy, cultural understanding, and friendship to stop a Third World War from unfolding?

In this political thriller, a computer error prompts an unplanned battle in the South China Sea between two superpowers with the potential to cause a Third World War.

ABOUT THE AUTHOR

Jeffrey Busch served in the Administrations' of United States Presidents Ronald Reagan and George H W Bush. He also served as United States Delegate to the United Nations in Geneva. He is a graduate of New York University in Business Administration and Emory University School of Law. He worked as a Press Aide to Mayor Ed Koch of New York City then as a Congressional Aide and Campaign Manager for Congressman Bill Green. He has been active in U.S. politics and International affairs for over 30 years .

Mr. Busch is the Founder of Safe Blood for Africa Foundation that established National Blood services in Africa and is credited with helping to save millions of lives. He also established Safe Blood for China jointly with the Ministry of Health of China. In addition, he established Club 25 International an organization operated in over 75 countries working with young adults to save lives with blood donations and to establish good citizenship.

Currently , Mr. Busch is Founder and Chairman/CEO of a billion dollar New York Stock Exchange Company.

He has worked extensively in China and met with hundreds of top officials in China.

Dr. Dominic Man-Kit Lam is a highly distinguisged Medical Professor formerly at Harvard Medical School and Texas Medical Center. He is also a world class artist, including having exhibitions at Grand Palais, du Louvre, Venice Biennale and Christie's, etc, as well as a well-known philanthropist who, with Dr. David Paton, first brought Orbis, the charitable flying eye hospital, to China in 1982 and founded other charity organizations. Moreover, Dr. Lam was invited to advise several Presidents in US & China, notably appointed by President George HW Bush as a member of the President's Committee on the Arts & Humanities. In recognition of Dr. Lam's many accomplishments he is often called the modern day Leonardo da Vinci.

Made in United States
North Haven, CT
23 November 2023

44445583R00189